WITCHING FOR CLARITY

PREMONITION POINTE, BOOK 4

DEANNA CHASE

ABOUT THIS BOOK

Clarity "Gigi" Martin moved to Premonition Pointe for a fresh start. And that's exactly what she got when she found her perfect haunted house on the seaside and a group of witches who welcomed her into their fold. It's not easy starting over at forty-one, but she's determined to do it on her own terms with her painful past left firmly behind her... until Sebastian Knight walks back into her life. Sebastian was the one person she'd ever trusted, but now it looks like he's the one who has been keeping secrets. After a ghost leaves a cryptic message for Gigi, she's determined to find the truth once and for all even if it means opening a Pandora's box of trouble.

When nothing is as it seems, Gigi needs to learn who to trust, or history is doomed to repeat itself.

CHAPTER ONE

"*I*'d rather get a cavity filled without novocaine rather than go on another date with the losers on this dating site," Gigi said, throwing her phone down on the couch in disgust.

"Oh, honey. They can't be that bad," Skyler, her neighbor, said, snatching her phone and scrolling through the recent matches.

"They are. And if you disagree, your standards are seriously compromised." Gigi stood and moved over to her French doors to stare out at the churning sea. It had been nine months since she'd divorced her abusive husband and moved into the lovely seaside home in Premonition Pointe. If it weren't for Skyler and the rest of her friends pressuring her to get back out into the dating scene, she'd have happily kept to herself, making her potions and spending quality time with her friends when they weren't too busy with their partners. Since she relished her freedom these days, she never felt like a third wheel… especially when Sebastian was around.

Gigi shook her head. If she were honest with herself, Sebastian was the main reason she'd agreed to let Skyler put her profile on Exclusive, the over-forty dating site for professionals. It was meant to match people who had similar lifestyles. Gigi found it pretentious, not to mention elitist, but Skyler had a point when he said the last thing that she needed was a gold digger hanging around. Gigi hated to admit it, but far too often when her dates realized she had money from a family trust, everything became about her bank balance and not anything else she had to offer.

Her ex had fit that description to a T, and now that she had distance from him, she could see the warning signs had always been there. It was better to date someone who already had his life in order and wouldn't only see her as his meal ticket.

It was too bad every single guy who'd messaged her on the app had been a pompous ass who led with his bank account balance instead of something interesting like what books he liked to read or his favorite hobbies besides the stock market.

"Wow," Skyler said, his eyes popping wide. "This one has a giant c—"

"Don't say it," Gigi said with a groan, clasping her fingers over her eyes. She'd forgotten about the one who'd sent her unsolicited dick pics. "I'm never going to get that image out of my mind."

"Why would you want to?" Skyler asked with a snicker, swiping to look at the next message. "This guy is hot. The one with the private plane."

"So is his wife," Gigi said dryly.

"He's already married?" Skyler asked with a gasp. "Does his wife know?"

"Yes." It had been quite a shock when his wife started messaging Gigi, too. Apparently, the couple liked to mix it up with multiple partners. And while Gigi didn't have any judgments about that, it wasn't for her. "I'm not much for sharing."

"Me neither," Skyler said, scrolling some more. "Damn. You weren't kidding." He tossed the phone down on the cushion and gave her a pitying glance. "And I thought the gay hookup sites were bad."

"When was the last time you were on a gay hookup site?" Gigi asked, raising one eyebrow. "Please don't tell me you and Pete have some sort of arrangement. If you do, I'm going to be convinced that romance is dead."

Skyler tossed his head back and laughed. "No, darling. Pete and I are monogamous. I think the last time I looked at one of those hookup sites was when we were helping Pete's co-worker make an appealing profile. You know, one that says hot, available, and interesting, but not desperate."

"Of course." Gigi's lips twitched into a small smile. "Did it work better than mine? Does this friend of yours have decent prospects? Or are they all rich douchecanoes like the ones that keep contacting me?"

"I don't know about rich, but there were plenty of douchecanoes. There always are. If you want to meet someone, there's always going to be sewage to wade through," he said, moving to stand next to her by the French doors and patting her arm.

"Nope." Gigi shook her head. "I'm swearing off dating. I've seen one too many penises this week. The worst was the one that had a hundred-dollar bill wrapped around it." She shuddered and made a face. "Talk about a narcissist."

"You know, I'm embarrassed to admit that at one time in my life, I'd have been turned on by that," Skyler said with a chuckle.

"That's TMI, Sky. TMI."

"Sorry!" He threw his hands up, flushing pink but grinning, letting her know he wasn't too mortified by what he'd said. "I sometimes forget you're not quite as open as my other friends."

"I'm open," she said, biting her bottom lip, feeling a little embarrassed herself. "I swear I'm not a prude, despite my preferences for leaving the dick pics to the bedroom and politely declining threesomes."

"Of course you are." He nodded, looking serious for once. Skyler had a penchant for humor and teasing. It was rare when he wasn't making a joke. "I just meant that some of my friends have zero filter. I didn't mean to imply you were uptight."

"It's fine," she said with a sigh. "It's just disheartening to get a look at the options out there."

Skyler tilted his head, making his stylish blond hair fall over one green eye. "Tell me again why you don't just go out with Sebastian? That guy is smokin' hot. How can you resist those smoldering gray eyes or his thick dark hair? Not to mention that chiseled jaw. And you do realize I'd kill to have those lips of his, right?" He touched his long fingers to his mouth and said, "Maybe I should make an appointment at the spa and see about some lip fillers."

"Stop." Gigi rolled her eyes. "You have no need for lip fillers. Besides, I'm fairly certain that Pete would not be on board with any cosmetic enhancements."

Sighing, Skyler nodded his agreement. "You're right. He's all about growing old naturally or whatever. Mr. All Natural would throw a fit if I modified anything." He smirked as he added, "But I bet he wouldn't be complaining when I wrapped my new and improved lips around—"

"Stop!" Gigi held her hand up, laughing at her friend. She

knew he'd only added that last bit to tease her after their earlier conversation.

"I was going to say popsicle," he said innocently, batting his long eyelashes at her.

"Sure you were."

They both laughed, and then Skyler glanced at the stairs. "Ready to face the past?"

Gigi's smile slipped from her face as she followed his gaze. She'd actually invited him over to go through a sizable portion of her wardrobe. She had a lot of designer clothes leftover from when she'd been married to James. He was the type of man who'd wanted his wife to look a certain way and dress to impress his country club crowd. It meant she'd shopped at all the high-end retailers and collected a number of expensive, well-made articles of clothing. Most of them were gorgeous, but they weren't anything she planned to wear again. They held too many memories she'd just as soon forget. Also, she was a beach girl now. Her current wardrobe consisted of peasant blouses, cotton skirts, and leggings with oversized shirts.

"We don't have to do this today," Skyler said, gently placing a hand on her arm. "We don't even have to do it at all. You can forget I ever even asked. I've already got a list of places to find used designer clothes."

"Like Always in Fashion?" she asked, referring to the new used clothing store that had just opened in town.

He clutched at his heart and stared at her in horror. "You can't be serious. Have you seen what they try to pass off as fashion in that place?"

"Jeans, sundresses, and graphic T-shirts?" she asked, raising one eyebrow.

He snorted. "That sounds about right, but no. Last night I

made a list of all the estate sales in the area. We could skip your attic and start bargain hunting instead."

Being a designer, Skyler had a passion for high-end garments, and when Gigi had mentioned she needed to do something with her collection, his eyes had lit up. He was in the process of opening his own boutique shop in Premonition Pointe and had been contemplating having a sister store for used designer duds. While Premonition Pointe was a relaxed beach town, it did have its fair share of well-to-do residents and tourists who would likely love bargain hunting while strolling through their quaint town.

"You know, I'd love to go estate sale shopping. Tell me when, and I'm there," she said with a smile. While Gigi was no longer interested in fancy clothes, she did love art deco jewelry and modern art.

"Perfect. There's one this Saturday at an estate about twenty miles down the coast. We need to get there early, so be ready to go by nine." He tapped something into his phone, no doubt putting the date on his calendar.

"Nine is early?" she asked, raising one eyebrow.

"Yes," he said, nodding his head seriously. "Anything before noon on a Saturday is sacrilege."

Shaking her head, Gigi started to make her way toward her stairs. "Come on. Let's get this over with."

Skyler jerked his head up and stared at her, his eyes wide with surprise. "You mean you're ready to face the past?"

She shook her head. "Nope. Just ready to let go of it one expensive garment at a time."

"That's my girl," Skyler said, hurrying to her side and slipping his hand in hers. "Just point me in the right direction, and I'll clear everything out. You don't have to do a thing, or even stay up there with me, if you don't want to. Just let your buddy Skyler take care of everything."

"I just might do that," she said as she sucked in a deep breath and took the first steps on her journey to not only rid herself of her past with her ex-husband, but also the one she'd left behind over twenty years ago.

CHAPTER TWO

*T*he narrow stairs creaked under Gigi's feet as she made her way up into the finished attic. It was a room she hadn't been in since the day she moved in months ago. A weak stream of light shone through the frosted glass window, illuminating the dust in the air, and the image invoked a strong memory of the attic in her childhood home. The one where she'd spent hours playing dress up in her mother's old theatre costumes. Gigi stood in the doorway with her eyes closed as she did her best to calm the suddenly rapid beating of her heart.

Thinking about her mother always caused mild panic attacks. She'd hoped that enough time had passed that she'd no longer feel like hyperventilating when she thought of the beautiful blonde with the infectious smile and tinkling laugh. It appeared all the therapy in the world wasn't going to help her overcome that particular response.

"Gigi?" Skyler said, pressing a hand to her shoulder. "Are you all right?"

She sucked in a breath of stale air and moved aside for him as she said, "I will be."

Skyler squeezed her shoulder in support, giving her an encouraging smile. "You can do this. Once I carry those overpriced, overworked, over-the-top garments out of here, just think how much freer you'll feel."

"Overworked? Overpriced? Who are you?" She laughed at him and felt most of the tension drain from her body. Leave it to Skyler to find a way to put her at ease when she was ready to jump right out of her skin. He was right. Once this was done, she would finally feel free from a life she never should've jumped into.

"Just your friendly neighborhood designer who doesn't take himself too seriously." He winked and walked over to a portable garment closet. "I assume most of the items are in here?"

"Most might be a bit misleading," she said with a sheepish smile and then waved a hand at a row of boxes.

Skyler's eyes lit up. "Gigi, did I mention how much I love you?"

"Only about a dozen times today." She grinned at him and then turned to a trunk, wondering what it contained. When she'd left her ex, she hadn't exactly been clear headed when she'd hastily packed up her belongings. All she'd wanted to do was leave that old life behind and move on in her new home by the sea. And she'd done that. Now it was time to let go of the past for good.

"Holy son of a biscuit," Skyler said from behind her. "You have a Bob Mackie?" His tone was hushed and full of reverence.

Gigi turned to find Skyler standing next to the portable closet. He'd unzipped the canvas and was holding a formfitting silver-beaded gown that she'd worn to a movie premiere a million years ago. The star had been a client from her ex's advertising firm, and he'd scored tickets when the partners had been otherwise engaged. "Yeah. It's only been worn once."

Skyler clutched his heart as he sucked in an exaggerated breath. "Gigi, my love, I'm about to die on the spot. You have no idea how happy you've made me." Suddenly his grin vanished as he clutched the gown and peered at her. "You don't want to keep this do you? I mean, I'd understand if you did, since it's just so... glorious. But this would make the most stunning window display for my grand opening. Of course, you probably don't want to give it up. Who would? I mean, an original Bob Mackie..."

"Sky?" she said, waiting for him to stop staring at the garment and look at her again.

"Yes?" His eyes were wide and full of longing.

"I don't want that gown. Anything you find is yours for the store. I already told you that. I have no intention of ever wearing that dress again. That night wasn't a pleasant memory for me."

"Oh. Right. Of course." He carefully placed the gown back in the wardrobe and gave her a sympathetic look. "I'm sorry. I should've realized you weren't attached to any of these things after what you've told me. I just... you know me and fashion. I get a little overwhelmed when staring at greatness."

She waved an unconcerned hand, trying to act like the unwanted memories weren't flooding her brain. Gigi didn't want to remember all the times she'd caved to James's demands. The way she'd gone along with the lavish lifestyle, over-the-top parties, and wasted money on things that had never mattered. They'd lived their life for show, as if having the perfect address or hottest designer on speed dial made them important. James had wanted to impress the Hollywood types, while all Gigi really wanted to do was spend time in her gardens and make friends with the ladies at her local book club. She'd wanted a quiet, normal life, while he'd wanted to hobnob with celebrities. Now that she was in Premonition Pointe, she had that life she'd always longed for. Only it wasn't a book club where she'd found her friends; it was the local coven. "Don't worry about it. That life is behind me now."

Skyler walked over to her and swept her up in a tight hug. "You aren't fooling me, Gigi Martin. I commend you for looking forward and carving out a new life, but pasts don't just fade away. No one knows that better than me," he said with a sardonic huff of laughter. "I'm not going to make you talk about it, but just know that I'm here for you and I understand. Got it?"

Tears sprung to Gigi's eyes. She hadn't had a friend like Skyler in many years. Not since she and Sebastian had been close back in high school. Sure, she had Grace, Hope, and Joy. They were great and she loved getting closer to them, but they didn't see through her the way Skyler did. It both warmed and shook her a bit. Still, she clung to him, grateful for his support, and said, "Thank you. You have no idea how much that means to me."

He pulled back and kissed her cheek. "I know what it means to live your life on someone else's terms. Thank the gods, I'm not in that place anymore. Pete is the first person who loved me for me and supports me in anything I want to do. It's my fervent wish that you find your own Pete someday."

She shook her head but smiled gently at him as she said, "I'm not in the market for my own Pete. Not now anyway. All I was looking for with that dating site was someone to flirt with for a while and maybe have some dinner. Too bad I couldn't even find that much. But it's okay, because I still have you. And your friendship is more than good enough for me."

The man who was always ready with a cheeky comeback and a teasing smile blinked back his own tears as he took her in his arms again. "Dammit, Gigi. I told myself I wasn't going to cry today no matter what I found in your closets, but here you've gone and turned me into a weepy fool."

She chuckled. "Oh, I'm fairly certain there's something in these boxes of mine that will still make you cry, so you were never going to last anyway."

Skyler laughed and pulled back. "You do realize that since you've moved in, you've turned into my favorite person, right?"

"Besides Pete," she said with a glint in her eye.

"Besides Pete." He nodded his agreement. "I knew five minutes after we met that we'd be besties."

"Same here. But that might've been because of the cupcakes you brought me as a welcome to the neighborhood gift." She winked at him.

"Someone had to take those damned things off my hands!" he said dramatically, pressing his hands to his flat stomach. "I was in danger of needing a whole new wardrobe."

"Like you need a reason to buy more clothes." They chuckled together and then went to work on collecting the garments he'd be consigning at his new shop.

After a few hours, there was only one trunk left. Gigi rolled her shoulders and then crouched down to open it. There was tissue paper lining the top, making Gigi frown. She didn't remember using any tissue paper when she'd packed her things. Curious, she moved the tissue aside and found her mother's preserved wedding dress. Gigi was immediately assaulted with vivid memories from twenty-three years ago.

Gigi stared, open-mouthed as she watched the large policeman escort Sebastian to the back of the car. A scream was stuck in her throat, and her entire body shook uncontrollably. Her life had just spun apart, and everything she'd held dear had shattered.

"You know I didn't do this!" Sebastian called back to her. "Gigi. Look at me."

At just eighteen years old, and with no one else in the world she trusted, Gigi met Sebastian's eyes.

"You know me. Trust your gut. You know in your heart that this isn't true." His gaze was steady, but there was no mistaking the pleading in his tone. Sebastian was scared. Of course he was. He was being arrested for the abduction of Carolyn Benson, Gigi's mother.

When the knock had come at the door, Gigi had thought the police were coming with news of her mother. Instead, they'd come for Sebastian because he was the last person who saw her on the day she'd gone missing.

Gigi opened her mouth to reassure him, to let him know that she knew they'd made a mistake, but nothing came out. Her words were stuck in her throat as she watched them stuff him in the car and take away the only person she trusted.

"Gigi? What's wrong?" Skyler asked, pulling her from her memories.

She blinked up at her friend, clearing her blurry vision. "It's my mom's wedding dress," she gasped out.

When Gigi was eighteen, her mother had just vanished one day, seemingly into thin air, and had never been heard from again. At first, Gigi hadn't worried much. Her mother was a photographer, and her job took her out of town often. Gigi had figured her mother had just forgotten to tell her she'd be gone for a few days. But when Gigi hadn't been able to get ahold of her, and her mother's employer had confirmed that Carolyn Benson wasn't on assignment, that's when Gigi's world had started to fall apart.

For an entire week, Sebastian, her best friend, had been by her side as the pair searched for Carolyn. They'd found her calendar and had tried to trace her steps the day she'd gone missing. Dentist appointment, grocery store, a meeting with her publisher, and then home where Sebastian had spoken with her for a few minutes when he'd come by to see Gigi. That was it. That was the last time anyone had seen her or her old VW Bug. They hadn't come up with a single viable lead as to what had happened to her.

Neither had the police, and that's when they set their sights on Sebastian, the boy from the other side of the tracks who'd admitted to speaking with her within an hour of her disappearance. And since he'd been home alone, he had no alibi. They'd pinned their circumstantial case on him and hauled him off to jail where he'd been berated for three days before a public defender had forced them to either charge him or let him go. With zero evidence against him, they'd had no choice but to let him leave.

But they'd spent the next six months hounding him and even going so far as to try to pin evidence on him. It was then that he decided that he could no longer live in that small town. He'd begged Gigi to go with him, but she couldn't. She'd been convinced that her mother would return, and she had to be there when that day came.

Only it never did. Instead, James was the one who'd been there for her and convinced her it was time to start living again. What she hadn't known at the time was that all he wanted was her trust fund. Life hadn't been especially kind to

Gigi over the last two decades, but she was bound and determined to change that.

"Holy shit!" Skyler said as he jumped back and pulled Gigi with him.

A shimmer of light caught Gigi's eye, and she froze as she watched the dress rise from the trunk seemingly of its own accord. The wedding dress filled out as if a body had slipped into it, then spun around, making the skirt flair out, showing off the pretty beading and delicate lace.

Then the dress floated across the room. One arm rose into the air and then letters started to appear in the dust on the glass window. Once the message was scratched in the dust, the dress suddenly dropped to the floor in a heap of fabric. Gigi moved forward and squinted her eyes as she tried to make out the hastily written message.

Skyler moved to stand beside her, holding her hand tightly in his.

"I can't make it out," Gigi said. "It looks like—"

"The one from your past has the answers," Skyler said in a hushed whisper.

Gigi let out a startled gasp, pain shooting through her heart and nearly breaking her as she realized what the message meant.

Sebastian had known what happened to her mother all along.

CHAPTER THREE

$\mathcal{S}$kyler blinked at Gigi as his face drained of color. "Gigi, did you know your house is haunted?"

She nodded, unconcerned about the fact that she lived with a few ghosts. She sometimes saw the Hannigan sisters. They'd made an appearance when she'd first purchased the place, though she didn't think either of them had animated her mother's dress. They would've shown themselves to her. But now she couldn't help but wonder who exactly had written that message. Was it possible her mother had just made an appearance? Her heart both ached and swelled with the idea. "Don't worry. The ghosts are friendly."

He glanced around as if one might suddenly pop up again. "Does that happen often?"

She shook her head. "Only when emotions are running high." In fact, the ghosts were mostly just a presence she felt but didn't really see often. And that was fine with her. The house had been owned by the Hannigan sisters and wanted someone who wouldn't displace them, so she felt a connection to them and was actually comforted that she didn't feel alone.

"Well... that's *interesting*, isn't it?" Skyler ran a hand through his blond hair and blew out a breath.

Gigi placed a hand on his arm, meaning to comfort him. "Don't worry. They aren't the sinister type."

He let out a nervous laugh. "I guess that's something to be grateful for."

"Yeah," she said absently, staring at the message in the dust and biting her lower lip.

"Do you know what it means?"

She turned to Skyler and nodded, unable to speak. How could she say out loud what she was thinking? That the person she'd trusted most in the world had betrayed her.

"WHO NEEDS WINE?" Grace Valentine asked, holding a bottle of Pinot Noir in the air. She was dressed in a smart black business suit and was wearing the fabulous blue stilettos she always wore when she had an important house showing. It was obvious she'd dressed to impress that day, but her put-together look was offset by her auburn locks sticking out all over the place due to her messy bun. She was sitting on a log around a small fire pit on the bluff overlooking the Pacific Ocean. It was the spot where the coven met at least once a month to brush up on their spell casting. But mostly they just drank wine and got caught up on each other's lives.

"Me," Gigi said, thrusting her wine glass in the other woman's direction. "Fill it up."

Hope Anderson, who was sitting to Gigi's right, chuckled and pushed her dark curly locks out of her eyes. The curvy event planner was vivacious and never failed to bring energy to their gatherings. She smiled at Gigi playfully. "Looks like someone has something they need to get off their chest."

"You have no idea." Gigi swallowed a few gulps of the wine Grace poured for her before turning to Joy Lansing, the tall actress who was sitting quietly on the other side of Gigi, thumbing through her phone. "Whatcha looking at, Joy?"

"Work emails," she said with an irritated sigh.

Grace raised an eyebrow. "Too many auditions and not enough time?" she teased.

Joy let out a bark of laughter. "If only I had that problem. You'd think with a hugely successful movie under my belt, that directors would be lining up to offer me at least small television roles, right?"

"They aren't?" Gigi asked her. "Looks like you've got at least some interest going on there if your mailbox is full."

Joy grimaced. "Sure, if I want to do menopause commercials or print ads for incontinence."

"Adult diapers?" Hope sputtered, barely able to contain her laughter. "You're kidding."

"Nope." Joy turned her phone around and showed them the email. "It says right here that they want someone to model these special 'urine collecting bottoms that are made to look like underwear.' Kind of like that period underwear I keep seeing advertised all over social media."

Gigi grimaced. "They want you to model underwear?"

"You're lucky you have such great legs," Grace said solemnly. "You could model underwear with no issues. I'd have to get some sort of cellulite treatment first."

"I'm not modeling incontinence underwear!" Joy said, looking scandalized. "That's almost as bad as appearing in an STI ad."

"Do they want you to do one of those, too?" Hope asked. "I hear the largest segment of new STI outbreaks are in retirement communities."

Joy pressed her lips into a thin line and shook her head. "No, thank the gods. But do remind me never to move to a retirement community."

"Oh, honey. You'll be fine. Just remember to use a condom and get tested regularly," Hope said, patting her friend's knee.

Gigi chuckled, enjoying the exchange between her friends. Contentment settled around her, making her feel both strange and happy at the same time. This dynamic was new for her. She'd never had a group of friends to lean on before and the more time she spent with them, the more she started to feel something mend inside of her that had been shattered years ago. The thought made her think of Sebastian again, and she involuntarily scowled.

"Whoa. What's that about?" Hope asked, reaching over and squeezing Gigi's knee. "You look like you're ready to murder someone."

Tears suddenly stung Gigi's eyes while her throat tightened. *Oh, gods,* she prayed to herself. *I can't fall apart like this. Not now.*

Joy sucked in a sharp breath as her body went rigid.

Gigi stared at the woman, watching with wide eyes as horror flashed over Joy's pale face. She reached out suddenly, grasping at the air, and then let out a choked sound before blinking rapidly.

"What did you see, Joy?" Grace asked gently.

Tears streamed down Joy's face unchecked as she turned to Gigi and grabbed her hand tightly in both of her own. "I'm so sorry, Gigi. I just… um, I just saw the moment when your mom was abducted." Joy glanced around the circle before meeting

Gigi's eyes again. "Did they ever find out what happened to her?"

Gigi's head started to spin as her heart sped up, making her feel like it was going to beat right out of her chest. "She was abducted? Are you sure? What did you see?" she choked out, having no doubt that her friend had really had a vision about her mother. She'd known all along that her mother must have been taken by someone. She would've never left Gigi like that. But this was the first time there had been any sort of confirmation. Hope and dread warred for dominance, making her chest ache even more.

"I…" Joy closed her eyes as if concentrating, and then when she opened them again, she turned to Gigi, but her voice dropped to a whisper as if she didn't want to put the words out into the world. "All I saw was a person larger than her, wearing a mask and gloves, come up and grab her from behind. The next image was the police arresting Sebastian."

Pain exploded in Gigi's chest. It was the first confirmation of what she'd known had to have happened to her mother. That didn't make it any easier to process, though. There was a small part of her that had always been on the lookout for her mother's beautiful blond hair and kind green eyes. Now even that small thread of hope had been snatched from her.

"Gigi?" Joy asked. "Are you all right?"

She squeezed her eyes shut and shook her head. That sharp pain that was always present when Gigi thought about that time in her life intensified, making her stomach cramp. It had been the single worst two weeks of her life. Her mother had vanished, and then her best friend had been arrested for her mother's disappearance. Ultimately, there hadn't been anything other than circumstantial evidence against Sebastian and he'd been released. But the missing persons case had never been solved.

And now after all these years, not only did she have confirmation that her mother had been abducted, a ghost had also told her that Sebastian had the answers. It didn't necessarily mean he was guilty, but it likely meant he had information he'd kept from her all these years. That knowledge made her want to scream with frustration.

"Gigi?" Joy prompted again. "You don't need to talk about this if you don't want to, but we're here for anything you need."

"She's right," Grace said while Hope nodded her agreement.

Gigi glanced around at them. Although talking about her mother wasn't something she ever did, for the first time in over twenty years, she felt the need to purge her soul. "It happened when I was eighteen," she said, staring at her clasped hands. "It was just me and my mom. My dad took off years earlier. One day, she was at the house, then a few hours later she wasn't. I never saw her again." Pain sluiced through Gigi, and it took every ounce of will she had to get out the next words. "She was never found."

"And Sebastian?" Joy asked.

Gigi gritted her teeth. "He'd come by the house to see me, but I hadn't gotten home yet. He was the last person to see her alive. The authorities automatically blamed him, but they had no evidence against him."

"Oh my," Grace said, her tone hushed. "That's… just about the most horrible thing I've ever heard." Her friend moved closer and wrapped an arm around Gigi's shoulders, pulling her in close. "I'm sorry, honey. No one should have to endure that. Not you or Sebastian."

"Sebastian," Gigi huffed out. "Right. That's what I thought

too until one of my ghosts told me he has the answers to what happened back then."

"You can't be serious?" Hope asked with wide, angry eyes. The wind picked up, tossing her black hair back, making her look like a wild witch, ready to take someone out. "You mean to say he's had information all this time and kept it from you?"

Gigi shrugged. "I guess so. I don't know how else to interpret the message. When Skyler and I were in the attic this afternoon, an invisible ghost animated my mother's wedding dress and wrote me a message in the dust. It said 'the one from your past has the answers.' Seems pretty straightforward to me since he's the only person around from my past."

"Maybe it's new information?" Joy asked, though she didn't sound convinced.

"If it was, why wouldn't he say something to me? It's not like he doesn't know where I live, right? Or that I've spent over twenty years wondering what happened to her." Gigi's anger was back now, and as far as she was concerned, that was a good thing. It was better to feel righteous indignation than crippling despair. At least her anger would propel her into action instead of making her want to curl up in bed for days on end. And since she had enough money that she didn't need to work, that was a real possibility.

Hope leaned forward, her expression set into determination. "You need to invite him over and pull the information from him. Maybe have a cocktail party at the house. Have the three of us there. I can try to listen in on his thoughts. Maybe Joy will have another vision. And Grace…" She trailed off, eyeing the third witch in the coven. "Well, she can maybe see if she can suss out which ghost was playing dress-up in the attic."

Gigi grimaced. "I don't think I want to talk to him about my mom with a bunch of people over."

"It won't be people," Hope clarified. "It will be us." She waved a hand around the circle. "And our significant others, of course, so it doesn't look like a weird ambush."

And Skyler, Gigi thought. She couldn't leave him out. If he saw all their cars in her driveway, he'd be wondering why he wasn't invited. She could do that, right? He already had the CliffsNotes version of what had happened. She'd filled him in after the incident in the attic. She cleared her throat. "So I just call him up and invite him over?"

Hope gave her a strange look. "Uh, yeah. Why not?"

"I don't want it to seem like a date," Gigi insisted. There'd recently been a time when she'd entertained the idea of going out with Sebastian. But that idea was long gone, and she didn't want him getting the wrong idea.

"It's just a cocktail party, Gigi. Tell him you're inviting friends over. That's it," Hope said.

"I know. It's just..." Gigi shook her head. "Never mind. I'll take care of it. Does Friday night work for everyone?"

They all nodded their agreement. Then Hope refilled their wine glasses and said, "Who wants to hear about the mother of the groom who got so drunk on champagne that she threw up on the bride just minutes before she had to walk down the aisle?"

"No!" Grace gasped. "Tell me that didn't really happen."

"I wish I could," Hope said, shaking her head. "The groom's mother just laughed and said now it was a Kinsington wedding and that according to tradition, the bride would be pregnant within the month. She said all of this while pouring herself another glass of champagne, which she then used for a prewedding toast." Hope let out a chuckle. "The best part is that the bride later announced that she was already pregnant and that if she ended up with twins, she was blaming her new mother-in-law."

"But what happened to the dress?" Joy asked, clearly horrified.

"Oh, that." Hope waved a hand. "Well, I saved the day of course. Turns out club soda really does work as long as you have a stain removal potion to go along with it."

"*You* cleaned it?" Grace asked, her blue eyes narrowed in suspicion. "That doesn't sound like you."

"It doesn't, does it?" Hope threw her head back and laughed. "That's why I charged a pain-in-the-ass fee. The extra funds are just enough to pay for the sex swing I bought a couple weeks ago."

"Sex swing?" the other three witches all said at the same time.

"What about Lucas's mother?" Joy asked in a hushed tone.

Lucas was Hope's fiancé, and his mother lived with them.

"Oh, she loves the swing. She uses it all the time."

"What?" Grace choked out a laugh. "Now I know you're messing with us."

Hope just grinned. "We call it the sex swing because that's what Bell called it when we brought it home. She said Lucas was conceived on one that looked just like it." Her eyes sparkled as she laughed again. "It's just a regular porch swing that we put out back, but now it's the sex swing."

"Hmm, maybe Owen and I need one of those," Grace said.

"Why? Are you planning on getting knocked up?" Hope teased.

Grace jerked back and then blinked at her friend. "Bite your tongue."

Hope snickered, and the rest of them joined in the teasing.

Gigi took a long sip of her wine and smiled to herself. This was what she loved about her new circle of friends. They were always at the ready to help in any situation, and no matter how awful it was, they always found a way to make her smile. Despite her trepidation about talking to Sebastian, she knew that whatever new information she gained, she'd be just fine with the three other witches by her side.

CHAPTER FOUR

*E*leven in the morning wasn't too early for wine, was it? Gigi stood on her patio and stared out at the churning Pacific Ocean with a glass of Chardonnay in her hand, trying to work up her courage to call Sebastian. Back at the cliff with her coven mates, she'd been convinced she could do this. But in the light of day, she was certain the lump in her throat would choke her and she'd end up sounding like a dying chicken.

"Just do it, Gigi," she scolded herself. What was the worst he could do? Say no? She shook her head, knowing the worst thing he could do was say yes. Then she'd have to face him. But dammit, she wasn't a coward, and she deserved answers. The fire in her gut flared to life, and before she could lose her nerve, she pulled out her iPhone and called him.

"Gigi," he said into the phone, his husky voice sounding slightly raspy as if he'd just woken up or he had a slight cold. It was sexy as hell and pissed her off immediately. He had no business piquing her interest like that. Not when he had information about her mother that he hadn't bothered to share. "It's nice to hear from you."

"Sebastian." She cringed when she heard her icy tone. That wasn't the way to convince a man to come to her impromptu party.

"Something wrong?" he asked.

Dammit, why did he sound so concerned? She was pissed at him and didn't care for the way he was already chipping away at her resolve.

Clearing her throat, she said, "Sorry about that. Just before you answered, I stubbed my toe pretty hard on the coffee table leg. I was trying not to let out a string of expletives."

"Oh, ouch," he said sympathetically. "Need me to come over and take care of it? I'm good with my hands." He sounded flirty now, making her grit her teeth.

"I'll be fine." Goodness, she was acting like an idiot. It was time to get it together. "But how about Friday night? I'm having an informal cocktail party of sorts and thought you might like to join us. Hope, Grace, and Joy along with their dates."

"Are you asking me to be your date, Gigi?" he asked, a smile in his voice.

"Um, no?" she stammered.

"It sounds like you're asking me to be your date. Is anyone else going to be there?"

"Skyler and his husband."

"Right. So it's a date. What time?" he asked, sounding pleased with himself.

She wanted to scream into the phone that he was delusional and that she'd never date him. Not now. Not after what she'd learned. But if she did that, she'd never find out what he knew. Even though it went against every fiber of her being to not shut him down, she forced herself to say, "Seven on Friday."

"Great. What should I bring?"

"Just yourself." *And a truck load of secrets and honesty*, she thought.

"Okay. See you then. And, Gigi?"

"Yeah?" she said warily.

"Thanks for the invite. I'm looking forward to it." The line went dead, and Gigi stood there staring at her phone for a long moment.

Her back door opened, surprising her, and she let out a small gasp as the phone flew out of her hand.

"Sorry!" Skyler called as he stepped out onto the patio. "I thought you heard me. I knocked on your screen door, but when you didn't answer, I let myself in. Good thing, too, cause it looks like I'd still be waiting for you out there."

"It's fine. I was just on a call." They were close enough friends that Skyler regularly walked in if the door was unlocked. Gigi focused on him, taking in his ripped jeans and old, faded George Michael T-shirt. She frowned at him. "What the hell are you wearing? And where are you wearing it to? A secret rave in an abandoned warehouse downtown?"

Skyler chuckled as he swept past her and leaned against the railing, the slight breeze ruffling his hair. "No, but that sounds promising. Got any E we can take with us?"

"Sure. Let me just dig it out of my breath mint tin," she said, rolling her eyes. But she couldn't help the smile that claimed her lips. Skyler was the one person who always lifted her mood within seconds of being in the same room with him. "You know, it's too bad you're gay. You'd make a great life partner."

His face flushed instantly.

"Oh. Em. Gee. Are you blushing? This is a first. I've never seen you blush before," she said, grinning at him.

"Stop," he said, waving an impatient hand. "We both know you'd bail on me after forty-eight hours. You'd probably OD on the Real Housewives franchise and threaten to choke me with a spoon or something."

He was right. She would have to strangle him if he made her watch too much reality television. "I'd be okay with marathons of Project Runway, though."

"And thank the gods for that. I'd have to find a new bestie if you weren't up for hours of Tim Gunn." He winked at her. "Now, tell me why you were looking like you were ready to murder someone when I found you staring out at the ocean."

"Sebastian. I'd just got done inviting him to the cocktail party I'm having Friday night. He thinks it's a date, but really I just want to get information out of him."

"Cocktail party? What? Why is this the first I'm hearing about it?" he demanded with his hands on his hips.

"Because I just decided to have it last night, and I was going to call you next. Do you think you and Pete can come?"

He pursed his lips and narrowed his eyes. "Well, I don't know. It's so last minute. I'll have to check my calendar."

"Don't make me hurt you," Gigi said, already knowing they didn't have other plans because Skyler had been complaining about the lack of events in his appointment book the last time they chatted.

Skyler pulled his phone out, sent a text, and then returned it to his back pocket. "Fine. We're in if Pete's up for it. Need me to bring anything?"

"Your fabulous charcuterie board? With candied almonds and ginger slices?" she asked hopefully.

"You're a piece of work, you know that?" he said, shaking his head even as he grinned at her.

"It's why you love me." She grinned back at him.

"Fine," he said with an exaggerated sigh. "I'll handle it, but you owe me."

"I always do. One day I might even pay up." She pulled him into a hug and whispered, "Thanks."

"Anything for you, babe." When he stepped away, he added, "Now get yourself together. We have somewhere to be."

Gigi glanced down at her long skirt and fitted white T-shirt. Then she eyed him. "Considering you look like you raided your teen wardrobe, I'm guessing wherever we're headed it's not exactly formal?"

"I never wore this as a teen." He raised his head and sniffed as if she'd insulted him. "If you must know, I was preppy back then, and the thought of ripped jeans was horrifying. I've since found the light. And thanks to Always in Fashion, I found this wonderful vintage T-shirt. Tell me this isn't fabulous." He waved a hand in a flourish, indicating she should study his look again.

"I thought you said you wouldn't be caught dead in that store," Gigi said, raising one eyebrow.

"So I lied. Sue me." He rolled his eyes playfully. "I actually went in to reassure myself they wouldn't be my competition, and that's when I found this fabulous thing. They have an incredible selection of vintage Tees. I'm almost a little jealous. Still, it's not the kind of thing I plan to sell, so I guess it's all right. Now what do you really think if my outfit?"

"I'm telling you, if those jeans were acid wash, you'd be a shoo-in for an 80s Madonna video."

"Really?" he asked, beaming. "That's just about the best thing I've heard all morning."

"You're too much." Gigi laughed. "Now, tell me my outfit is fine for wherever we're headed."

He eyed her for a moment and nodded. "Just grab your checkbook and your keys, and let's go or else we're going to miss it."

"Miss what?" she called as she disappeared inside to grab her bag.

"You'll see." He followed her, and once she was ready to go, he slipped his arm through hers and said, "Come on, Rapunzel, let's blow this castle and have some fun, shall we?"

Gigi happily let him lead her out of her house and was grateful he'd arrived to take her mind off Sebastian. She shook her head. No more thoughts of him. She was headed out on an adventure with her new best friend. And she couldn't wait to see what he had in store for her.

CHAPTER FIVE

"*W*here exactly are we going?" Gigi asked as she squinted at the winding road in front of them. They were headed through a thick patch of redwoods, away from the coast. "You're not taking me into the forest and forcing me to hike five miles again, are you?"

Skyler scoffed. "Would I be wearing my favorite Gucci sneakers if I was going to go traipsing into the woods?"

She glanced down at his feet that were clad in beige and maroon colored tennis shoes. Sure, they looked brand new, but if it weren't for the Gucci logo on the side, she never would have guessed they cost almost as much as rent on a small apartment. "I'm guessing that's a no. I'm glad to hear it," she said with a chuckle. "So? Where is our final destination?"

Skyler grabbed a folded piece of paper from the console of his Lexus SUV and handed it to her. "This, my friend, is where we're going to find some fabulous treasures."

Gigi unfolded the paper and scanned the advertisement. It had a picture of a large Victorian on a perfectly manicured lot with directions on how to get to the estate sale. The doors were opening in fifteen minutes. "Ah, I see. Is this the one you told me about a few days ago? I thought we were supposed to go on Saturday at the crack of dawn."

"Nope. That's a different one, and I still expect you to go even after your rager on Friday night."

She laughed. "The last time I was at a rager, I left at ten thirty after James drank so much that he didn't even recognize me. I was kind of hoping he'd pass out there and give me some peace, but somehow, he ended up in a cab and I ended up taking care of his ass for two days after. I haven't felt the need to attend a rager since then."

"Gigi," Skyler said, shaking his head. "Don't take this the wrong way, but your ex is shit."

"No kidding," she said with a sad shake of her head. "I should have left a lot sooner, but it just wasn't that easy. He was a master manipulator."

"Don't beat yourself up about it," Sky said. "You're not the only one who has found herself in a shitty situation. Sometimes it takes a while to figure out how to change it. But you have, and your life is fabulous now. So fabulous that you're with me, headed to an estate sale with a pocket full of money and no one to answer to but yourself. Sounds great right?"

"You can say that again," she said, making a concerted effort to put all thoughts of her ex behind her. Nothing good ever came from thinking about him. Instead, she focused on the task at hand. "How did you hear about this sale? I thought the one this weekend was the only one happening for at least a few weeks."

"This one showed up in my email box first thing this morning. The door opens in fifteen minutes, and the email listed designer garments," he said with a reverent sigh. "Some from Alexander McQueen."

"Oh, goodness," Gigi said, grinning at him. "Jackpot."

"I just hope I'm the first one in the door," he said, pressing on the gas and taking a corner at a speed that made Gigi uncomfortable. She grabbed onto the edge of the seat and pumped the imaginary brake out of reflex. He glanced over at her and chuckled. "Relax, babe. I used to race cars when I was younger."

"You did?" Gigi's eyes widened, and she wondered what else she hadn't yet learned about her neighbor.

"Yep. Used to go down to the track with my brother and his best friend, Jake. I was good enough that I won a few races, but it was too expensive. Besides, I was just there to ogle Jake."

"Did he play for your team?" Gigi asked, chuckling at her friend.

"Not at the time, but when we ran into each other a few years later when my totally masc, straight brother wasn't around, he didn't hesitate to take me up on my offer to go back to my dorm room." He gave Gigi a wicked grin. "I swear if he hadn't still been friends with my brother that we'd have had a salacious long-term love affair."

"Sounds like the time you put in at the track paid off after all." Gigi winked at him. She really enjoyed her time with Skyler. His stories were always entertaining, even if she did suspect he embellished at times. Who cared? He was fun and great at getting her out of her house, where she was in danger of becoming a recluse if left to her own devices. She'd spent too many years hiding away from the world. After the trauma of losing her mother and then enduring her controlling husband, it had taken her a long time to come into her own. But when she'd kicked her ex's ass and left him last year, she finally felt the sweet taste of freedom. There was no going back. Not ever.

Ten minutes later, Skyler made a turn into a long driveway lined with trees. When the driveway opened to a clearing, Gigi let out a gasp when she saw the house. It was even more magnificent in person. "How old do you think this place is?"

"Pretty sure the advertisement I read said the family had it built back in the mid 1800s." He put the car in park and hopped out. Before Gigi even had her seatbelt unbuckled, he had her door open for her.

"Thanks." Warmth spread through her at the attention. It was nice to be taken care of for once. Her ex hadn't been very chivalrous after they'd gotten married. In fact, it was like a switch had been flipped and he'd turned into someone completely different once he had a ring on her finger. Gigi sighed and followed her friend toward the gorgeous Victorian.

"What was that all about?" Skyler asked curiously.

"Oh, just remembering all the times my husband never opened a door for me." She pasted a smile on her face. "I'm not saying that's the reason I kicked his ass and dumped him, but it sure didn't help his case."

Skyler tossed his head back and laughed. When he sobered, he looked her in the eye and said, "I wish I'd been there that day. That douchebucket deserved to have his balls ripped off. You're worth all the time and effort in the world, Gigi. Remember that and never settle for less."

Her skin tingled with something that felt like magic. It wasn't that he was putting a spell out into the world; it was more like she could sense that Skyler was a kindred spirit of sorts. "It sounds like you've had some experience with abusive partners."

He nodded. "Just once. It was the man I was involved with before Pete. Man, was I a complete mess, too. I got out of that relationship, but I honestly thought I would never date anyone again. It wasn't that I didn't think I deserved to have someone; I just didn't trust anyone." He gave her a shy smile as he added, "But Pete was just there, and so effing patient with me. It's like he took my walls down piece by piece without me even noticing. Then one day, there was no turning back. We were together, and I couldn't imagine not spending my life with him." Skyler's solemn expression turned to one of mischief. "Poor bastard. Imagine having to put up with my shenanigans all the time."

Gigi slipped her arm through Skyler's and held on. "I can only imagine it would be wonderful. Now let's go inside and find some treasures."

Skyler turned his gaze to the house, nodded once, and then led Gigi up the steps. Just as they got there, the door opened on its own, revealing a wide grand hallway with stairs to the right that curved up to the second floor.

"Wow," Gigi said, taking in the gleaming wood floors and the ornate garden tapestries on the wall. "This is even more impressive than I imagined."

"Same. I was expecting—" Skyler stopped mid-sentence when a butterfly from one of the tapestries materialized in real life and fluttered toward them. The electric blue beauty fluttered its wings a few times before heading down the hallway. When neither Gigi nor Skyler moved, the butterfly backtracked, repeated the fluttering, and once again made its way down the hall.

"I think we're being summoned," Gigi said in a hushed tone.

Skyler was standing stock-still, apparently unwilling or unable to move. His eyes were wide when he asked, "Do you think it's safe? I don't want to end up on the evening news with a headline that reads *Witch and Her Gay Best Friend Die After Searching for Heirlooms*."

Gigi took a moment to breathe in her surroundings before answering. Ever since she'd moved into her house, she'd been able to sense the mood of places. The Victorian was no different. While there was a low buzz of energy in the hall, it wasn't unwelcoming. Just slightly heavier than she was used to, likely due to the age of the home. There was more history, more layers of human emotion. She glanced down the hall where the butterfly had disappeared and spotted a faint outline of white light, almost like a glow. As soon as she blinked, it was gone again.

"It's fine, Sky," Gigi said, taking a step forward and nudging him along. "Trust me. Whatever or whoever is waiting for us has the energy of Glinda the Good Witch."

He snorted. "You mean we're going to find a witch who is all smiles and pleasantry but won't exactly do much to help us until we're seconds from death?"

Gigi couldn't help but laugh. His assessment of Glinda from *The Wizard of Oz* wasn't exactly far off. "It's better than being whisked away by flying monkeys, isn't it?"

"I'd rather we don't have to endure either scenario if you don't mind," he said haughtily.

"It's a deal. I'll let you know if this place starts to give off a dangerous vibe, and if so, we'll leave immediately before the tornado kicks in."

"Deal."

They walked cautiously down the hallway until they came to a set of wide-open doors that led to an elegant parlor that took Gigi's breath away. The entire western wall was floor-to-ceiling windows with a spectacular view of a garden fit for royalty.

"Look at that settee," Skyler whispered reverently. "Royal blue velvet Louis the XV-style loveseat with hand carved legs.

It would be perfect in the dressing room of the store. Just perfect."

"It's for sale," a woman said, appearing out of nowhere. "Let me get you a price sheet."

Gigi glanced around, wondering where the pixie-sized woman who appeared to be in her early thirties had been hiding. Behind the door? Under a desk? In the closet? All of the options seemed unlikely since she'd have noticed someone emerging from all three places.

"Oh. My. Prada." Skyler pressed a hand to his chest and gazed longingly at a garment rack that was on the other side of the room. "Do you see that, Gigi? The gorgeous white wool suit? It looks like the one Carly Preston wore in *My Favorite December*. The one she wore to the New Years' Eve bash when she finally got together with Archer Riveria." He let out a swoon-worthy sigh and floated over to the rack without waiting for her answer.

Smiling to herself, Gigi focused again on the tiny woman searching through the papers on a small writing desk. Her hair had been cut and styled into a cute 1950s pageboy style. The teal and black polka dot rockabilly dress she wore with her high heeled Mary Jane shoes was the perfect outfit to compliment her look.

"Found it," she said and pulled a piece of paper out of a folder with a flourish. "Whew. I was afraid that I'd lost it for good this time." She gave Gigi a sheepish smile. "You know how you put something away so you can find it easily next time?"

Gigi nodded, enjoying the bubbly energy wafting off the woman.

"Yeah, that's what I did here, but it seems every time I put something away, finding it is dicey." She laughed. "You'd think

I'd learn and just leave the important things out where they're impossible to miss."

"Maybe you have a ghost who keeps hiding things," Gigi said without thinking. "That's what happens in my house." Gigi cringed internally. She hadn't meant to bring up her ghosts. It was something she usually kept to herself and her small circle of friends because so many people were still skeptical. But even though they'd barely spoken, Gigi felt a natural ease with the woman in front of her. It was almost as if she knew her, but that was impossible. Gigi would remember if they'd met before.

"Ghosts." She nodded thoughtfully. "It's entirely possible. This wouldn't be the first time I've encountered one." She held her hand out. "Hi, I'm Autumn."

"Gigi." Their hands touched, and a comforting warmth spread through her.

Autumn's hand tightened around Gigi's and she held on for a moment longer than normal as Autumn stared in wonder at her. Then she blinked, dropped Gigi's hand, and took a step back as she cleared her throat. "Welcome to the Thorne estate sale. Are you looking for anything in particular or just treasure hunting?"

"Garments in particular," Skyler called from his place over at the clothing rack. "But I want to see everything. You never know what you're going to find."

Autumn stared at Gigi for a moment longer before turning to Skyler and smiling. "Perfect. When you're done there, let me take you upstairs so you can see the rest of Mrs. Thorne's wardrobe."

"There's more?" Skyler breathed, his face alight with excitement.

She chuckled. "Yes. The garments you're looking at are just

a sampling." Autumn walked over to him, introduced herself, and the two of them got lost in a conversation about all of Mrs. Thorne's favorite designers.

Gigi watched them for a few minutes before slipping out of the room and following the arrows to a large sitting room in the back of the house. It had obviously been the formal living room with an attached dining room. The walls were covered in wood paneling, and there was a more modern white couch and two matching armchairs facing each other. But the end tables and china cabinet were the same Louis the XV style as the settee from the other room. It was clear the owner had gone for chic comfort while trying to keep the rest of the furnishings as original as possible.

"I knew you'd come," an ethereal voice called from behind her.

Gooseflesh popped out over Gigi's skin. She froze before carefully turning in the direction of the voice. At the head of the table in the adjacent dining room, there was a shimmering outline of a woman wearing an elegant beaded gown. Her curly hair was piled up on her head with tendrils framing her face and showing off teardrop diamond earrings. She held up a gloved hand and beckoned for Gigi to come closer.

As if in a trance, Gigi moved forward, both drawn to the woman but also terrified because she knew that face. She'd seen it before in a black and white photo in her mother's things.

"You know of me, don't you?" the woman asked.

"Yes," Gigi said. "You're my great aunt Celia." Gigi had gotten used to being around ghosts at her own house, but the materialization of a relative in a house she'd never been to before was starting to freak her out. "What are you doing here?"

The ghost let out a humorless laugh. "Enjoying my home before that twit Garrison Thorne, Jr. sells it for the cash that he'll waste on bad business deals and even worse investments."

Gigi racked her brain, trying to remember what she knew about Celia. Not much. "You lived here?"

Celia nodded. "My entire life. It's too bad Branson and I never had children. If so, the house would've never fallen into my cousin Tillie's hands. The only thing she was good at was decorating. At least she passed that on to her great granddaughter. Vanessa Thorne had great taste. She sure made it pleasurable haunting this old place the last several years."

"Wow. I don't know much about this side of the family," Gigi said, taking a seat at the table, content to keep talking to her ancestor for as long as she could. The truth was Gigi didn't know much about any of her ancestors. She had some photos from her mother's things, but nothing from her father at all. He'd left before she was old enough to even remember him. "Do you have more living relatives around here?"

The ghost shook her head. "Garrison and his gold-digging trophy wife are only related by marriage. Neither are worth your time."

"Oh. That's unfortunate. But that's okay. You're obviously here to tell me something," Gigi said, narrowing her eyes at Celia. "Otherwise you wouldn't be using that much energy." The light around Celia had started to dim, and Gigi could tell the ghost would be fading away soon. Most couldn't materialize for a long period of time. It appeared Celia was at the end of her energy cycle.

"I am. I like that you're a smart one." She smiled at Gigi and then sobered. "Listen carefully now because this is important. Trust doesn't come easily, but if you don't earn it, history will repeat itself."

Gigi's body stiffened as she felt her insides turn to ice at the warning. Leaning forward, she stared at the fading light of the ghost and asked earnestly, "Earn whose trust?"

The ghost opened her mouth to say something, but before she could get any words out, she vanished.

Tears of frustration stung Gigi's eyes. History will repeat itself? What the hell did that mean? Gigi couldn't help but think the worst. Her mother had disappeared, and her case had gone unsolved. Did that mean her abductor was back and someone else would be harmed?

Sebastian's face materialized in her mind, and she felt sick to her stomach. Had the authorities been right all those years ago?

No.

The word was loud in her brain, but she had no idea where it came from. Her subconscious? Celia? All she knew was that deep in her gut, she didn't believe that Sebastian had anything to do with her mother's disappearance. And if there was one thing she'd learned in her forty years, it was that when she listened to her gut, it never steered her wrong.

Sebastian. He was the key. The one from her past who had the answers. Friday couldn't come soon enough.

CHAPTER SIX

"*T*hired Autumn today," Skyler said as he placed his charcuterie board on her counter.

Gigi placed a stack of napkins next to the plates and looked up at him. They were in her kitchen doing the last-minute prep for her cocktail party. "You did? For what?"

"He wants her to be his assistant at the boutique," Pete said, snaking an arm around Skyler and pulling him close. Skyler glanced up at his husband and gave him a small smile as Pete added, "And it's not a moment too soon either. I've barely seen this one since I got home. He's been so busy he even missed dinner last night."

"Sky!" Gigi exclaimed. "The dinner Pete spent all day working on for you?"

"I got a call from a private client who needed something to wear to an event! I couldn't say no." He squeezed Pete. "I'm sorry, honey. But I made it up to you later, right?"

Pete's eyes gleamed as he gave his husband a mischievous smile. "Yes, you did, baby. Who cares about dinner?"

Skyler chuckled. "That's what I thought. Dinner was still excellent warmed up for brunch this morning."

A small stab of pure jealousy pierced Gigi in the chest as she watched them. She couldn't remember a single moment in her marriage when she and James had been even half as in love as her two friends were. Their joy just radiated off them, and while she loved seeing it, she also couldn't help but feel just a little sorry for herself.

All those years she'd wasted on James, who'd turned out to be not just a disappointment but an abuser on top of everything else. He'd only raised his hand to her that one time, but the emotional abuse had been there almost from the beginning; she just hadn't recognized it for what it was. And that, more than anything, pissed her off. He'd been so charming that she'd overlooked far too much. Now that she was free, it made her almost sick to her stomach to remember how much garbage she'd put up with over the years before she'd finally walked away. Gigi had filed a police report about the attack, but he'd skipped town and she hadn't heard from him since. As far as she was concerned, that was good enough for her. If she never heard from him again, it would be too soon.

"The party can start now!" Hope called as she waltzed into the kitchen carrying a case of champagne. "Who's ready for some bubbly?"

"I am." Skyler's hand shot in the air.

Pete shrugged one shoulder and said, "Sure."

"Excellent." Hope place the box on the counter, smoothed her fitted suit jacket, and glanced around. "Where are the champagne flutes?"

"In the dining room," Gigi said. "On the table where you put them earlier." Hope had planned the party and had taken care of most of the details earlier that day.

"Right," she chuckled. "Forties brain. That's what I've been calling it when I have a mental lapse. It's better than imagining I'm getting early onset dementia." Glancing at Skyler she said, "Can you stuff these in the refrigerator? I'm gonna go fill those glasses."

"On it." Skyler got busy with his task while Gigi grabbed the charcuterie tray and followed Hope into the adjoining room. She'd just finished setting the rest of the food on the table when the doorbell rang.

They both glanced up and stared at the door across the room.

Hope raised an eyebrow. "It has to be Sebastian. Everyone else would've just walked right in, don't you think?"

Nerves made Gigi's throat tighten, making it impossible to answer Hope. Instead, she just nodded and forced herself to cross the room. She'd never been nervous about seeing Sebastian before, but now that she was certain he was hiding information from her, she was both angry and full of trepidation. If he really was withholding something he knew about her mother's disappearance, there was definitely a reason, and likely one that was going to gut her.

Taking a deep breath, she opened the door and did a double take when she spotted Autumn, the woman from the estate sale who also happened to be Skyler's newest employee. "Uh, Autumn. Hi," Gigi stammered, feeling like an idiot. Why couldn't she seem to keep her composure that evening?

Autumn peered past Gigi, looking nervous. "Am I early? I thought Skyler told me to be here at seven?"

"No! You're not early," Skyler called as he hurried over to

them. "You're right on time actually." He gently nudged Gigi to the side and then pulled Autumn into the house. "I'm so glad you could make it." He turned to Gigi. "You remember Autumn, right? I told her she should stop by so she can meet Pete and get to know some people in town since she's relatively new around here."

Gigi didn't miss the slightly apologetic look he sent her for inviting someone she didn't really know to her fake party. But she had someone else she needed to focus on, and worrying about Autumn wasn't on her radar. "Of course I remember Autumn. Go introduce her to Pete and grab her a glass of champagne while I—"

"Hey, Gigi," Lucas, Hope's fiancé, said as he walked in. He wrapped her in a quick hug and gave her a kiss on her cheek. "Thanks for the invite. Hope's been talking about this party nonstop for three days. You'd think she hadn't seen her girls in weeks," he added with a chuckle.

"You know how excited we get," Gigi said with a nervous chuckle of her own.

He raised one eyebrow as if he knew they were up to some sort of shenanigans. Of course he did. Hope would've told him.

Gigi waved him off toward Hope. "Your better half is over there pouring the champagne."

"Then that's exactly where I need to be." He winked at her and crossed the room toward where Skyler was introducing Autumn to Hope.

Voices sounded from behind her, and she spun to find the rest of the crew walking in, chatting and laughing. She said her hellos to Grace, Owen, Joy, and Troy. They were all easygoing and happy to be gathered for an intimate party with their closest friends, and it didn't take long for her to relax and join the conversation.

"Gigi, did you know that Carly Preston has a really

impressive herbal room?" Joy asked her, referring to the famous actress who was Premonition Pointe's newest permanent resident. She was holding a small white, unmarked jar in one hand and a champagne glass with the other.

"No. I didn't know that," Gigi said. "Is she a collector or a practitioner?"

"Definitely a practitioner." She held up the jar in her left hand. "I told her you have a gift with herbs, and she actually wanted me to give you this to see what you thought of it. It's supposed to help smooth out cellulite."

Gigi frowned as she looked down at her own legs peeking out from the hem of her fairly casual cotton dress. "Was this her way of telling me I might need a little work done on my thighs?"

"Oh goddess, no!" Joy said, sounding horrified that she might have offended Gigi. "Your thighs are perfect as near as I can tell... I mean, of what I've seen of them." She let out a nervous laugh, and Troy, who was standing beside her, couldn't hold in his own chuckle.

"Good job, babe," he stage-whispered. "Way to give your friend a complex."

"Stop." She playfully swatted his chest. "Go talk to Skyler about that photoshoot you two are supposed to be setting up next week. I don't need your help here. I'm perfectly capable of putting my foot in my mouth all by myself."

He laughed again, pressed a kiss to her temple, and winked at Gigi as he strode across the room to chat with the designer.

"Sorry!" Joy said, giving her an apologetic smile. "That didn't start out well. Carly is an amateur herbalist. She works on potions and herbal remedies to relax after spending so much time on set. This salve though, she thinks might be marketable, and she wanted to get your opinion before she decided to do anything."

"Like a professional opinion?" Gigi asked, shocked.

"Yeah."

"But I'm not a professional. I don't sell anything I make," Gigi insisted. It was true that she had a gift with herbs. Ever since she was young, Gigi had felt a connection to the earth and the magical plants she produced. And she made everything from lip balms to eye creams to headache potions. She'd once had ideas of opening a shop, but being married to James had killed that idea. He'd wanted her to be available when he needed her for his own business needs. She'd agreed at first, imagining that at some point the tides would shift and she'd have her turn at a career. But when it became clear all he cared about was money, Gigi had put her dreams aside, knowing that if her business ever became anything substantial, he'd take it all from her one way or another.

"You should," a familiar husky voice said from behind her.

A tingle of anticipation started in Gigi's stomach. *Sebastian.* She turned and spotted her old friend, hating the way she was immediately drawn to him. He had information he'd kept from her. She should be wary of him, not want to wrap her arms around him and melt into his embrace.

Dammit.

"Hi, Sebastian. Glad you could make it." She put her hand out, intending to shake his, but he just grabbed it and pulled her into the hug she'd been longing for. Both of his arms slipped around her, tucking her close. There was no stopping it. She pressed her cheek into his chest, breathing in his woodsy scent. The world slipped away and for a moment, it was just her and Sebastian, back in their treehouse in the woods, keeping each other safe.

"Sebastian!" Lucas called. "It's good to see you. I didn't know you were going to be here."

Gigi slipped out of Sebastian's arms and took a step back as Lucas put his calloused hand out to shake Sebastian's. There was no hugging this time as the two men shook and made small talk.

"I hear you're going to be here for at least the summer," Lucas said. "Got time for some hiking? I could really use a trail buddy."

"Absolutely," Sebastian said with a nod. "Since I'm taking a little hiatus from the courtroom, I've got plenty of time. Just let me know when and where. I'll be there."

"Excellent. Let's set up a time for next week."

Gigi watched as the two men made plans and wondered if she should warn Lucas. But warn him about what? That Sebastian had information about her mother's disappearance but hadn't told her? That somewhere in the far dark corners of her mind, she feared that Sebastian had some part in her mother's disappearance? It couldn't be true. She just needed to get him talking. "Sebastian," she said, slipping her arm through his. "I hate to interrupt, but there's something I want to show you."

"Of course." He placed his hand over hers and gave Lucas a nod. "Thanks for the invite. I'm looking forward to it."

As Gigi led Sebastian toward the French doors that led outside, she glanced over her shoulder at Lucas. He gave her a thumbs-up, and she wondered what exactly he was up to. Surely Hope had told him what this evening was really about. Why had he asked Sebastian to go hiking with him? This wasn't the time to find out. She had recon to do.

After leading him outside to her patio, she stood at the railing, staring out at the ocean. The energy of the house was the reason she'd purchased it, but she'd be lying if she said the view wasn't a close second. The time spent near the ocean filled her well and centered her. She supposed that was why she brought Sebastian outside to have this conversation.

"Nice party," Sebastian said, his gaze trained on the churning sea below them.

"Thanks." She glanced over at him, taking in his gorgeous profile. Sebastian had a strong jawline and gorgeous silver eyes. Normally he was cleanshaven, but that evening he had a sexy five-o'clock shadow.

His lips curved up into a seductive half smile as he turned to her, clearly aware that she was staring.

Gigi averted her gaze, trying to pretend she wasn't imagining what it would feel like to rub her cheek against his.

"So, Gigi, what is it you wanted to talk to me about?" he asked.

Her gaze snapped back to his. "What makes you think I wanted to talk to you about something?"

He chuckled and gestured to the house. "Maybe because you have a house full of people, but the moment I got here, you dragged me outside where no one else could interrupt us. Don't forget, Clarity," he said, using her given name, "I know you. We might both have more years and a few wrinkles on us now, but neither of us have changed that much. Something's on your mind. I can tell by that line right here." He touched her forehead lightly with one finger.

Gigi let out a frustrated sigh, hating that he knew her so well. There really was no beating around the bush about this. He'd see right through her. "I need you to tell me everything you know about my mother's disappearance."

CHAPTER SEVEN

*S*ebastian blinked at Gigi, surprise flashing in his gray eyes. He glanced over at the French doors again and then back at her. "That's why you changed your mind about seeing me again? You think I have information about your mom?"

Gigi narrowed her eyes, wondering if any of his surprised reaction was an act. At any other time in her life, she'd have said no. But now... after the message from the ghost in her attic? She really wasn't sure. "Don't you?"

He shook his head and mumbled something inaudible as he turned to head back into the house.

"Sebastian, wait," she called, unable to let him leave until they talked this out. "Please. Can you just tell me what happened that day when you came by the house?"

He paused, held still for a couple of beats, and then sighed as he turned around and walked back to her. "There isn't anything new that I didn't tell you then."

"Okay," she said, nodding. "I believe you, but would you

mind humoring me? I… well, I just feel like I'm missing something."

He frowned. "What is this about? Is there a new lead in your mom's case?" he asked.

Gigi closed her eyes and shook her head slowly. "No. It's not that. Not really. I've just been… getting this feeling that I need to look at what happened with fresh eyes. I can't keep burying it and pretending I'm fine. Because I'm not."

"I see," he said softly, reaching out and draping an arm over her shoulders.

Gigi stiffened for a moment, but when he pulled her into a hug, she let him, unable to resist the physical comfort. It was a weird juxtaposition with her body welcoming his affection while her head screamed no. After a few seconds, she pulled away and crossed her arms over her chest.

Sebastian placed his hands on the railing and stared out at the horizon. "That was the day I was supposed to give you a ride after our last class, but I was held up by Mr. White because he wanted to talk to me about being a TA for his class the next semester. By the time we finished the meeting, I was an hour late meeting you at my car. You'd left me a note that you were going to take the bus. I immediately drove to your house to apologize, but you weren't there."

"I was at The Apothecary, trying to get a job," Gigi said, remembering that while she'd been walking to the bus, she'd slipped into the herbal store and noticed a help wanted sign. She'd spent the next two hours talking to the owner and proving her worth as an herbal specialist.

"Right. Your mom didn't even realize you hadn't come home yet. She actually told me you were in your room, but when I went to find you, it was obvious you hadn't been home that afternoon. When I went back to let her know you weren't there, she was pacing the kitchen floor, muttering something about stale coffee and bad come-ons."

Gigi smiled sadly. Her mother had been a coffee junkie. She must've gotten the new lazy barista who didn't care if he was serving hours-old coffee and spent way too much time hitting on her.

"When I told her you weren't home," Sebastian continued, "she jumped as if I'd startled her. After she seemed to collect herself, she told me I could wait for you, but I declined and told her to let you know I'd stopped by and to have you call me later. I had a paper to write. Then I left. That's it."

"That's it?" Gigi asked, sounding skeptical to her own ears even though she hadn't meant to. It was just so unusual for Sebastian to not wait for her, especially after he'd stood her up. "You just left?"

"Yes," he said defensively. "Your mom was clearly agitated. I thought it was better to give her space, and I had work to do. What was I supposed to do, just wait indefinitely? For all I knew, you'd left with James and wouldn't be home for hours."

The words hung in the air between them. James had been a sore subject between them back then. Sebastian hadn't liked him and hadn't been shy about his feelings. At the time, Gigi had thought he was upset because she didn't have as much time to spend with him, but now it seemed clear that it was more than that. Sebastian had been jealous. How had she not realized that back then? Gods, she was a fool sometimes.

When Gigi didn't answer him right away, a muscle in Sebastian's jaw pulsed from the tension he was holding. He stared down at his hands and seemed to consciously unclench his fingers from the railing. "Never mind. That was a long time ago. The fact is I wish I *had* stayed. If I had, who knows what would've happened? Maybe things would have turned out differently. Instead, I left and didn't return until you called the next morning because your mom never came home."

"Are you sure that's it?" Gigi asked again. He hadn't said anything she didn't already know, and that was the problem. Because of the ghost's message, she was certain there was more. "You're one hundred percent positive she didn't say anything else or you didn't see anything else unusual?"

"I don't know what to tell you, Gigi," he said, his eyes looking sad. "You obviously think I know more than I do, just like everyone else in Bellside." Shaking his head, he moved toward the door. "You know, there's a reason I left that tiny town way back then. I thought that was behind me. I thought you at least believed me, otherwise I never would have decided to stay here. Do me a favor, will you?"

Gigi felt small, embarrassed by her obvious distrust of the person she'd leaned on the most back then. How could she be doubting him now, after all these years? The ghost's words echoed in her mind again, making it so that she couldn't ignore the message. There was no denying that Sebastian had some knowledge that would lead to what happened to her mother. And she wasn't going to give up until she found that missing piece of the puzzle, even if it ripped her heart out while doing it. "What's that?"

"Let those people in there form their own opinions of me." He nodded to the house. "I don't deserve to go through what I did back home." Without waiting for her reply, he strode away from her and back into the house.

Gigi watched him go, her stomach aching as she wondered if she should've just told him about the ghost's message. Though she wasn't sure how that would help, considering his story of what had happened that day had never wavered. Why would he suddenly come up with new information just because a ghost had left her a message?

Frustrated with both her exchange with Sebastian as well as the ghost's cryptic message, she went back inside to try to make amends with Sebastian. But the minute she stepped back inside, everything went wrong at once. The door slammed shut from a burst of wind, smashing her index finger between the door and the frame.

Gigi let out a cry of surprise and whimpered when she realized her finger was trapped.

"Holy hell, Gigi," Sebastian said, striding back toward her. But Owen got there first, quickly freeing her finger from the door.

With her finger throbbing, Gigi hurried toward the hall bathroom, needing both the sink to clean her wound as well as the first aid kit. But when she reached for the doorknob, it fell off in her hand, making it impossible for her to enter the bathroom. "Dammit."

"Are you okay?" a woman asked from behind her.

Clutching both her finger and the doorknob, Gigi spun around, frazzled and feeling out of control. Autumn was standing there, concern in her expression. Tears of complete frustration stung Gigi's eyes, and she hated herself for it. Why, after all those years of holding herself together, never letting James get to her, was she falling apart in her own house just because she and Sebastian were at odds?

"Um, I smashed my finger in the door, and now I'm locked out of the bathroom where the first aid kit is," Gigi said, holding the doorknob out for the younger woman to see.

Autumn reached for the doorknob, pausing slightly to ask, "Do you mind if I try it?"

Gigi let out a small hysterical laugh. "No. Not at all."

Her small hand closed over the doorknob. Autumn studied the end of the knob for a moment then lined it up and turned. The door opened without any trouble. Gigi glanced between Autumn and the knob before reaching out to test it. It turned right and left, and when Gigi pulled on it, the knob stayed in place just like it was supposed to. "How did you do that?" she asked Autumn, a little awed.

Autumn shrugged. "Luck?"

"Whatever it was, I'll take it." Gigi stepped in, reached under the sink for the first aid kit, and placed it on the counter.

While Gigi ran her finger under cold water, Autumn opened the first aid kit and pulled out the antiseptic.

"Here," Autumn said, holding out a towel for Gigi.

Gigi did as she was told and let the other woman take care of her until her finger was cleaned and bandaged. "Thank you," she said, amazed at how comfortable she was with the virtual stranger. "Were you a nurse in another life?"

Autumn chuckled. "Not that I know of." She closed the first aid kit and stowed it back under the sink. "I did babysit a lot as a teenager, so fixing up a few scrapes isn't exactly new territory."

A vision of Autumn sitting on a couch with her arms around two young girls as they read from a book flashed in her mind, and Gigi was certain the vision had actually happened. It just felt so real. "I bet you were really fantastic at it, too."

"I did okay. The two little girls I took care of were the sweetest, and I miss them a lot, but they don't really need me anymore."

Two girls. Gigi had been right. It wasn't the first time she'd had a vision that had been true, but usually they weren't that accurate or confirmed that quickly. "Do you still get to see them ever?"

"No. They live a couple of hours south of here. But I keep in touch with their mom on social media, so I see a lot of secondhand updates. They're doing well."

"I bet that's hard," Gigi said as they exited the bathroom and headed back to the party. "Is that why you moved up this way?"

"Yes, and sort of? I actually moved because this is where the job was until Mrs. Thorne passed away."

Gigi's eyes widened. "You actually worked for Mrs. Thorne?"

She nodded. "I was the house manager for about five months. But now that the estate sale is over, the heirs don't really need me anymore, so I was let go. You and Skyler came along at the perfect time. I can't wait to dig in and start working on his store."

"I didn't really have anything to do with it," Gigi said. "I don't work with Skyler. We're just good friends."

Autumn glanced over at her new boss. "Huh. I got the distinct impression that Skyler thinks you'll be helping him for the foreseeable future."

"Oh, that. Sure," Gigi said, smiling. "I imagine I will do whatever he asks. I don't have a job, so pitching in gives me something to do."

Autumn glanced around at the house, let out a low whistle, and then nodded approvingly at Gigi. "You're life goals."

"What?" Gigi laughed nervously. "What does that mean?"

Autumn shrugged. "It means I admire your life. Single woman living in a fabulous beachfront home, best friends with a famous designer, and well off enough to not *need* to work. What's not to love?"

Gigi gave her a wry smile. "Well, Autumn, I haven't always been this person. Some of my life choices have been... questionable. I'm rectifying them, but the truth is, I wouldn't be in this position without a lot of help from a family trust. It helped me walk away from a bad marriage and also gave me time to heal so I could decide what I want to do instead of what I have to do."

"See? Life goals," Autumn said with a decisive nod. "I've also had a bad relationship, only mine hasn't gone away yet. He just keeps coming back like a bad rash."

Gigi placed her hand on Autumn's arm, offering support. "You don't have to engage with him, you know."

Autumn nodded. "I don't answer his calls, but sometimes he just shows up where I am. It's creepy, but he's sly enough that I don't have anything concrete to go on if I filed a restraining order. I can't keep him from public venues."

With a racing heart, Gigi tugged Autumn down to sit on a nearby couch and said, "Autumn, I hope I'm not overstepping, but my experiences in life make it so that I can't ignore this. That type of behavior is very dangerous, and I want you to know that no matter what, you can always call me for help. *No matter what.* If you need someone to come just be with you wherever you are in public or if you just need someone to talk to, I'll be here. You can call me at any time. Three in the morning. Whatever."

"That's—" Autumn's voice cracked, and she cleared her throat. "Thank you."

"Hand me your phone," Gigi said gently. "I'll put my number in your contacts."

Autumn did as she was asked, and when Gigi handed her phone back to her, she blinked back a few tears.

Gigi squeezed her hand and said, "I understand. I really do. Now let's go drink some more champagne and forget about that jackass for a while. There's no chance he'll end up here."

"Thanks again," Autumn whispered as they crossed the room to join the rest of the group.

"Hey," Sebastian said, coming up from behind her. "How's your finger? Is it okay?"

She nodded. "Autumn took care of me." She reached for one of the champagne bottles, only to realize it still needed to be uncorked. After tearing off the foil, she got busy twisting the metal cage and then the bottle to loosen it from the cork. Only the harder she tried, the less success she had. The cork refused to budge despite her best efforts, and in no time, she was sweating from her attempts.

"Need help?" Sebastian asked.

"Yes, please," she said, handing him the bottle.

He checked her work with the metal cage and then started to turn the bottle. Within seconds, the cork popped and everyone cheered. He shrugged one shoulder. "Looks like you were just seconds from finishing the job."

Only she hadn't been. The cork hadn't budged at all. She eyed his hands, wondering if he had magic fingers. "Well, maybe so, but I appreciate the help."

The rest of the evening, everything Gigi touched went wrong. She broke three glasses, locked herself out on the deck, slipped in the kitchen and bruised her elbow on the counter, and then finally, while she was saying goodnight to her guests, she got her hair caught in the security chain on her front door.

"Really? You've got to be kidding me!" she cried as pain radiated down her neck.

"Since when did you become so clumsy?" Sebastian asked, reaching out to gently untangle her hair.

She glanced up at him. "Just tonight it seems."

"Seems like you pissed off the karma gods or something."

"I guess so."

Sebastian smoothed down her hair and then took a step back. "There. You're free."

Gigi glanced around, noting that everyone was gone except for Sebastian. "Thanks. Um, I guess I'll see you around?"

His lips quirked up into a teasing smile. "You're throwing me out?"

"No, I..." She blew out a breath, frazzled by the events of the night. "The party's over. I just assumed you were headed out like everyone else."

"I'll help you clean up," he said and strode back over to the table where there was a pile of empty glasses and used plates.

Gigi followed him and, true to form, as soon as she reached for a couple of the empty champagne glasses, she tripped on absolutely nothing and knocked half a dozen of them over. One flew off the table and smashed at her feet.

"That's it!" Gigi threw her hands up in the air. "I give up. Have I been cursed or something?"

Her skin started to tingle as if someone were standing behind her, and the faintest voice whispered, "Sebastian doesn't have the answers you're looking for."

CHAPTER EIGHT

"What?" Gigi spun around, adrenaline running through her veins.

There was no one there.

Gigi turned to Sebastian. "Did you hear that?"

He frowned as he glanced around. "I heard something, but I couldn't make out the words."

A wave of pure relief washed over Gigi as she processed the message from one of her ghosts. The message from the attic hadn't been referring to Sebastian. All of her suspicions and angst of the last few days had been misguided. "Holy shit," she muttered and shook her head as she grabbed one of his hands with both of hers. "I owe you an apology."

His eyebrows shot up. "How's that?"

"I think we need to sit down."

"Let's go." Sebastian grabbed her hand and led her to the couch in her living room. He sat in the corner and then patted the cushion.

She sat willingly, and when his arm slipped around her shoulders, she leaned into him just like she had all those years ago. Tears of relief pricked her eyes. This was the one place she'd ever felt safe. When she'd thought he'd been keeping information from her, the thought that she'd never truly had someone on her side had nearly broken her. Her body started to tremble, and she wrapped her arms around herself, trying to calm all the emotions taking over.

"It's okay, Gigi," he whispered. "I promise. Whatever is happening, I'm here for you. I've always been here for you."

There was no stopping the tears that rolled down her cheeks. She'd spent years estranged from him, using the excuse that she had to stay away from him because of her husband. And then when she'd ditched James, she'd still kept her distance because the past wasn't something she'd been able to face. It hurt too much. But here she was, forced to deal with it by a rogue ghost. She wouldn't deny herself his comfort any longer. She couldn't.

Gigi turned into him, burying her face into his chest. "I'm sorry."

"You don't have anything to be sorry for," he said, caressing her back lightly with his fingers.

"Yes, I do," she forced out as she pulled away to look up at him. "I was given a message by a ghost here in the house and made assumptions about you that turned out to not be true. I didn't trust you, and you didn't deserve that."

His eyebrows pinched together as he frowned. "What message?"

She sat up straighter, trying to get herself together, and told him about the message from the attic.

"So someone from your past has the answers to your mother's disappearance, and you thought that someone was me?" he asked, sounding astonished.

She nodded and looked away, too embarrassed to meet his

gaze. "You're the only person in my life right now from my past."

Sebastian reached out and gently turned her face so that she had no choice but to look at him again. "I can understand why you might reach that conclusion. Don't beat yourself up about it. How about I help you find out who the ghost is talking about?"

"How?" she asked.

He shrugged. "I don't know. Make a list of everyone who was in your life at the time, and we'll see if we can track them down." Sebastian gave her a reassuring smile. "I do have resources for that sort of thing."

Since he was a lawyer, she had no doubt that he did. Why hadn't she just talked to him first?

Trust.

That was the problem. It was the major problem and also the key ingredient to figuring out the mystery of her mother's disappearance according to yet another ghost. And without it, history would repeat itself. A shiver ran through her, and no matter how much she wanted to burrow and hideaway from everything like she had been doing her entire adult life, it was time to face it. Both for her mother and herself.

"You don't mind?" she asked. "I don't want to be a burden."

He gazed down at her, his eyes piercing hers. "Gigi, you have never been a burden. Now stop overthinking this and just say thank you."

Her lips curved up into a small half smile. "Okay. Thank you."

"You're welcome." He pulled her into him, giving her a long hug.

When she finally pulled away, she got up and disappeared into her office to grab a notebook and pen. On her way back to the living room, she stopped in the powder room to wash her face and give herself a pep talk. Looking in the mirror, she said, "No more crying. No more falling apart in front of Sebastian. Got it?"

Her eyes were red and slightly puffy. It had been an emotional evening, leaving her drained, but she was going to see this through. Sebastian was her best shot at finally getting to the bottom of her mother's disappearance.

After returning to the living room, she once again sat next to Sebastian and opened the notebook. "Okay, time to list everyone we remember who might know anything about what happened to Mom."

"Your next-door neighbor?" Sebastian asked.

"Liza?" Gigi's eyebrows shot up. She was the older neighbor next door who'd looked out for both of them. Gigi couldn't imagine she'd held anything back from her or the detective when they'd interviewed her, but Gigi wasn't going to rule anyone out. Maybe she had new information or hadn't thought a detail was important.

"Yes. What's her last name?"

"Liza Crane. But she must be in her eighties by now."

"I'll check," Sebastian said, taking the notebook from her and writing the name down.

"My mom's boss. Ricky something. He managed the magazine she worked for," Gigi said, frowning as she tried to remember his last name. "Ricky Kemp? Kent? Something like that."

"What magazine?"

"*Central Coast Secrets.*" It had been a travel magazine highlighting the small tourist towns on the Central California coast. Gigi wasn't even sure if it was still being published.

"Got it," he said, making another note. They went through a

dozen or more names of people in Bellside that Gigi and her mother both knew, no matter how insignificant they were. Like the yoga instructor from their weekly class as well as the manager at the local café who'd had an obvious crush on Carolyn.

"We have a lot of people here without last names," Sebastian said, rubbing his jaw.

"Will that make it impossible to trace them?" she asked, leaning back into the couch.

"Not necessarily. The firm has access to PIs that can find just about anything, but it will cost us."

"That's fine. I can afford it."

Sebastian glanced around the house and nodded. "Looks like money isn't a problem."

"Family trust," she said with a humorless chuckle. "After knowing how I grew up, would you ever have guessed there was a trust out there that contained the kind of money that would put me in a beach house and—"

"Attract a man who was only interested in your investment accounts?" Sebastian asked bitterly.

Gigi blinked up at him, her mouth open, shocked at his bluntness.

"Sorry, I—"

She started to laugh, cutting him off. "Please. Don't be. You're only speaking the truth. If I'd left the money untouched, perhaps I'd never have wasted all those years on the jackass of the century."

Sebastian wrapped his arm around her shoulders and pulled her into his chest again. He kissed her temple and said, "I'm sorry. If I'd stuck around, maybe things would've been different."

"How's that?" she asked, curious about what he meant.

Would he have seen through James and warned her, or was he referring to the attraction they'd always had for each other that had run just below the surface? The attraction neither of them had been brave enough to confront back then.

His gray eyes flashed almost silver as he stared down at her with an intensity that made her blood pressure spike. After a moment, her gaze shifted to his full lips, and all she could think about was how many times she'd daydreamed of tasting him.

Sebastian's hand came up, and he gently caressed her cheek before clearing his throat and saying, "You needed someone back then. If I'd had the courage to stay, maybe that someone would've been me."

Gigi reached up and placed her hand gently over his. "Don't do this. You know I needed you, but you needed to take care of yourself, too. That town… if you'd stayed, they'd never have stopped harassing you. Besides, I was already dating James. It's not like I would've listened if you'd told me he was a user who deserved a swift kick in the balls."

"No? Why's that?" he asked. "Didn't you trust my judgement?"

She snorted out a laugh. "I should have. Trust me when I say I will now. But back then? No one could've told me anything. James has charisma in spades and is really good at making a person feel like they are the center of his universe. It's intoxicating… until it isn't, and then you realize he's just a controlling asshole who will say or do anything to get his way. I was too young and inexperienced to know better."

He pursed his lips, contemplating something that he didn't voice. Instead, he gently brushed his thumb over her bottom lip and said, "Ever since I kissed you that night when I brought you home about a month ago, I've been wanting to do it again."

Her breath caught, but even though she'd had the same thoughts, she didn't say anything. She just kept her eyes on his and unconsciously licked her lips.

Sebastian let out the faintest of moans. "If you do that again, I'm not going to be able to refrain from tasting you."

She felt her lips twitch up into a tiny smile as she darted her tongue out, running it over her bottom lip.

"Don't say I didn't warn you." He moved in, gently brushing his lips over hers. But the moment they touched, hunger swept through her and she opened for him, turning their sweet kiss into something hungry and slightly desperate.

"Gigi," he whispered.

"Yeah?" she said, running her fingers down the back of his neck.

"I want to take you upstairs and finally find out what I've been missing all these years."

The bluntness of his statement shocked her. This attraction was something they'd always been careful to step back from. But damned if she didn't want him, too. And the fact that she was forty-one and no longer a clueless eighteen-year-old meant that there was no reason to say no. No reason to keep her distance. It was time Gigi finally got what she wanted for a change.

Without a word, Gigi stood and held her hand out to him.

He glanced up at her, his eyes glinting again, but also holding a question. Was she sure? They both knew this would change things. It wasn't as if they had a close friendship these days, but they'd been very close at one time, and it would be easy to fall for him. Did she even want that?

No. She wasn't in the market for any sort of serious relationship.

But as she looked down at him and felt his hand tighten on

hers, she didn't care about what might happen in the future. Right then, all she wanted was Sebastian.

"I'm sure if you are," she said, answering his unspoken question.

"I've never been surer of anything in my life." Sebastian rose from the couch, picked her up in one swift motion, and carried her upstairs, all while kissing her with everything he had.

CHAPTER NINE

*D*espite the obvious passion raging through Sebastian, Gigi was surprised when he gently set her on her feet at the edge of her bed and moved away slightly, letting his forehead rest against hers. His warm breath mixed with hers, and the quiet intimacy of the moment made her heart swell and thump harder against her ribcage.

"Sebastian?" she asked.

He brought his hand up, caressing her cheek gently. His lips curved into a whisper of a smile as he said, "I just needed a second to savor this moment."

"Damn," she breathed, closing her eyes as a swell of emotion washed over her. "You're going to wreck me, aren't you?"

"In the best possible way," he said as he lowered his head, claiming her lips again.

Gigi melted into him, letting herself be completely consumed by his tender touch. As he ran one hand down her back and buried one in her hair, she knew she was taking a leap into something that would never leave her unscathed. And in that moment, she was more than willing to sacrifice the heart she'd tried to protect for far too many years.

With trembling hands, Gigi reached for the buttons on his shirt. Sebastian stilled and watched as she slowly worked his shirt open and pressed her palms to his well-defined chest. His muscles twitched under her touch, and his skin felt better than anything she'd ever imagined.

Sebastian shrugged out of his shirt. She let her eyes roam over his body, unabashedly admiring him standing there in just his trousers. When she met his gaze, she said, "You're the most beautiful man I've ever seen."

He gave her a sexy half smile as he reached for her, gently grabbing her by the waist and pulling her in close to him. "And just how many naked men have you seen, Clarity?"

She didn't miss his use of her given name, but for once she didn't feel the need to correct him. He was the one person who really knew her, *really* knew her, and it just felt right in the moment. And although his question embarrassed her, she answered anyway, knowing there could never be secrets between them. "Including you?"

He chuckled. "I'm not naked yet."

"Yet," she said, smiling up at him. "Once I get the rest of your clothes off you, the answer is two."

He raised one eyebrow. "Really?"

"James was my first and since we divorced, I... Well, there hasn't been anyone since."

"Jesus, Clarity," he said, his voice husky. "And you think I'm the one who is going to wreck you?"

Gigi started to shake her head, but Sebastian's mouth came back down on hers, and he kissed her with so much passion all her protests vanished. Her world narrowed to him and the passion sparking between them.

Sebastian took his time, slowly but deliberately exploring every inch of her, making her come alive under his touch. His strong, capable hands did something to her, healed her, made her forget there was ever anyone before him. By the time they were under the covers together, Gigi felt as if she'd waited her entire life for that moment with him.

He hovered above her, staring down at her with half lidded eyes, all sex and heat, but also tenderness and emotion. And when they finally joined together, Gigi knew he hadn't just wrecked her; she was shattered in the best possible way.

Hours later as Gigi lay in Sebastian's arms, her head resting on his shoulder, she said, "Wow. That was... unexpected."

He kissed the top of her head and chuckled softly. "That's not how I expected the evening to end, but I can't say I'm disappointed."

She lifted off him slightly so she could meet his gaze. Everything inside of her screamed to keep the moment light, to not share that she'd been turned inside out by his tender touch that had been combined with raw need and emotion that had touched her deep in her soul. But when he reached up and brushed a lock of hair out of her eyes, there was no stopping the words from tumbling out of her mouth. "Is it always like that?"

His brows pinched together as he asked, "What do you mean?"

Gigi let out a small, humorless huff of laughter and lowered herself back down so that she didn't have to keep looking him in the eye. She'd been sure they'd shared a rare connection, something that didn't come around every day. But what did she know? She'd only been with one other person. It was just her bad luck that he'd never made her feel as if one touch could make her burst into flames. But it wasn't just the passion that had made the night so incredible. It was the fact that he'd made her feel as if she was the most beautiful and precious person on the planet. Like he'd relished pleasing her as if her pleasure was his own.

She shook her head, disgusted at herself for romanticizing what they'd shared. They had a night together. Nothing more. That was obvious. "If you don't know, then I guess that's my answer."

Sebastian's hand slid up her bare back and tangled lightly in her hair while he used his other hand to caress her cheek. Then he whispered, "No. It's never like that."

"What?" Gigi stilled, barely able to even breathe as she waited for him to elaborate.

"You asked if sex is always like that, right?" he asked as he sat up, bringing her with him and lifting her chin so that she had no choice but to look him in the eye.

Gigi nodded, unable to form any words.

"It's not. Not even close." His gaze dropped to her mouth as his tongue darted out and licked at his lower lip.

"Is that good or bad?" she asked, shaking now.

It was his turn to let out a humorless chuckle. "Both, Clarity. Both."

"Why?" she breathed, her heart pounding.

"Because, baby, if this relationship we're starting goes south, you're not the only one who's going to be wrecked."

A slow smile curved Gigi's lips, and a burst of joy ran through her. "So it's not just me. There's a connection here, right?" She pressed her hand to his chest and then to hers, right over her heart.

"An incredible one," he agreed. "And in my forty years, I've only ever felt it with you." Before Gigi could say anything, he captured her lips again, pouring every ounce of his emotion into the kiss, until she was once again lost in him.

* * *

"WELL, WELL, WELL," Skyler said as he swept into Gigi's house holding two paper cups and a bakery bag from Pointe of View Café. "Just look at you. You're glowing." He handed her one of the coffees, his eyes sparkling with mischief.

"I'm not glowing," she muttered to herself even as her cheeks grew warm. From the way Skyler was looking at her with his knowing expression, she was certain he knew Sebastian had stayed the night. There was no getting out of it. He'd have the story out of her within two minutes once he started probing.

Skyler took a long sip of his coffee before rolling his eyes at her. "Girl, if you were glowing any brighter, I'd need sunscreen."

His playful tone made her chuckle, and she decided to just own her happiness. "All right. So it was a good night. I deserve that, right?"

"Just good?" he asked with a raised eyebrow. "Tell me that man is better than just *good*."

Her cheeks grew hotter, but she ignored her reaction and nodded. "Yes. Better than good. Much better in fact. Three times better."

"Three times. Damn, lucky you." He winked and headed into the kitchen where he sat on one of the barstools. After pulling out two donuts, he handed her a maple bar.

Gigi took a bite and moaned when the sweet goodness hit her tongue.

"Stop. I don't need to know what you sound like when you're rolling around with Sebastian all night," he teased.

"Please. You're probably one breath away from asking me what his penis looks like. Modesty just isn't your thing."

Skyler threw his head back and laughed. "You're right about that. But I'll try to tone it down a touch." He gave her a wicked smile when he added, "I just have one question."

"Gods," she said with a sigh, wondering how she could gracefully get out of this conversation. But she knew it was impossible at that point, so she just went with it. "Just one more question."

"How was the morning sex? Tell me he woke you up with his big—"

"Skyler!" She put a hand over his mouth, stopping him. "I'm not giving you those kinds of details. A girl has a right to her secrets." Then she narrowed her eyes at him. "How did you know Sebastian stayed over? You're never up that early."

"You're right. I'm not. But Pete was. He was out watering his flower garden before the sun came up. He gave me the dirt. Said you two looked like you were going to get down and dirty right there against your boytoy's SUV."

This time Gigi's entire body heated with embarrassment. She'd followed him out to grab the newspaper that was lying in her driveaway and couldn't resist kissing him one last—okay, a few more times, before letting him go.

"Oh, honey," Skyler said, squeezing her hand. "There's nothing to be embarrassed about. In fact, I think we should celebrate. Mimosas and a fancy brunch after we hit this estate sale. What do you say?"

"Deal."

"Perfect. Now finish your maple bar and let's go before the rest of the vultures show up."

The Saturday estate sale was held just south of town at a large mid-century beach house that wasn't unlike the one Skyler and Pete lived in next door to Gigi.

"Do you know what you're looking at here?" Gigi asked as she stood in front of the house, her eyes on the views behind it. The house sat on a bluff overlooking a cove that was filled with rock formations that were being battered by the churning sea.

"Artwork and jewelry," he said. "There might be some clothes, but it didn't sound promising."

"Lead on." Gigi followed him into the posh home. The marble floors gleamed beneath the pristine white couches and natural wood mid-century furniture. It was very high end, and Gigi had no doubt that they'd come across some interesting items.

A woman in a red suit with her blond hair styled in a French twist approached them, her black heels clacking on the floor. "Hello," she said, sweeping a disapproving eye over Gigi, unable to hide her sneer.

Gigi almost laughed as she looked down at her gray linen crop pants and flip flops. She wasn't exactly dressed for high-end society. Skyler wasn't any better in his ripped skinny jeans and faded Frankie Goes to Hollywood T-shirt.

"Good morning," Skyler said, his voice higher than normal and laced with a bit of an edge. He'd noticed the woman's judgment and was not amused. "We're here to take a look at the estate jewelry. Can you point us in that direction?"

"Oh, you'll need to wait until I have the time to show it to you personally." Her voice was filled with fake sweetness. "We can't just leave a collection like that lying around. You know how it is."

Skyler's lips pursed as if he'd just eaten a lemon. He sucked in a deep breath, and Gigi knew he was about to eviscerate her.

"Yes, I do," Gigi said, forcing a fake smile as she held out her hand in front of her, showing off the two-carat, art deco diamond-and-sapphire ring she always wore. Her grandmother had left it to her years ago, and even though Gigi wasn't one for wearing expensive jewelry, she almost never took it off because she knew how much her grandmother had loved it. She just felt closer to her with the ring on. "This one time I was at an estate sale where a ruby necklace went missing, and it was a huge scandal because when the investigation was over, we all found out the curator had lifted it and six other pieces that she blamed on the estate shoppers."

"What?" The woman automatically reached up to finger the ruby drop pendant she was wearing.

Gigi eyed it and then smiled at her. "That's what I said. One would have to be really stupid to steal from their employer, wouldn't they?"

The woman narrowed her eyes at Gigi and said, "I don't really care for what you seem to be implying."

"That's funny," Gigi said flippantly. "Because I didn't really care for your snap judgment of us based on how we're dressed. If you'd bothered to ask us anything before making assumptions, you'd have learned that Skyler is an accomplished designer who is opening a store in Premonition Pointe. We're here because one half of his shop is going to stock upcycled items from high-end designers. He was looking for vintage stuff to stock his store. As for me, I've donated most of the stuff in my attic and am just here for the entertainment. Only I didn't expect to run into such a snob. If you're too worried about us stealing the jewels, it's probably best if Skyler and I just move on to the next estate sale."

Without waiting for the woman's reply, Gigi slipped her arm through Skyler's and started to lead him back toward the front door.

"Skyler Cole?" the woman called after them, her voice in a slight panic.

Skyler let out a small chuckle before turning back. "The one and only. It was... interesting to meet you... I'm sorry, I didn't catch your name while you were judging our casual attire. But I guess it doesn't matter now, does it?"

Gigi didn't bother to hide her laugh as she tugged him onto the front porch.

"Wait!" the woman pleaded as she ran after them. "I didn't mean to offend anyone. Truly. It's just that at the last estate sale, a few pieces did walk off, and ever since then my boss has been on me about making sure I don't trust anyone. It wasn't personal, I swear. I'm Candy."

Candy? Gigi shook her head. Of course that was her name. Gigi rolled her eyes, but when she realized the woman was about to cry, most of Gigi's schadenfreude disappeared. Conflict and drama were two things that Gigi tried to stay away from because she always walked away feeling awful. Life was too short for that nonsense. The woman had just gotten the better of her this morning.

"Please, come back in, and I'll set you up to take a look at the jewelry collection. I also have a small closet full of designer clothes if you want to check that out, too."

Skyler glanced at Gigi with one eyebrow raised, still looking put out by her attitude.

Gigi shrugged a shoulder. "Doesn't hurt to take a look, right?"

"I suppose." He eyed the woman. "Next time don't be such a judgmental snobzilla, all right?"

Candy swallowed and nodded once before quickly turning on her heel and guiding them to the study that was just off the great room that overlooked the ocean.

Gigi let out a little gasp as soon as they entered the white wood-paneled space. There were books lining one wall from ceiling to floor while the three others were filled with art. It was visual overload in the extreme, but she couldn't help but be delighted when she spotted an original Jackson Pollack on one wall and a Georgia O'Keefe on another.

The estate manager strode over to a locked case and opened it for Skyler. Gigi barely glanced at the jewelry. Instead, she went straight to the paintings, admiring the details while wondering exactly whose estate they'd stumbled on. But when she went to ask, Candy's phone rang and she excused herself.

"Should I start shoving jewels in my pockets?" Skyler scoffed before bursting out laughing. "My god, Gigi. You really let that snob have it. Honestly, I didn't even know you had that in you. What happened to my sweet neighbor who's only caustic about her ex?"

Gigi gave him a rueful smile. "That was my humble roots showing through. Before I learned about our family trust, I never knew we had money. Mom never told me. So that was a surprise. We lived on her photographer's salary, which could be tight sometimes. Honestly, I have no idea why she didn't touch the money in the trust to make life easier, but I suppose she had something to prove to herself."

Skyler eyed her curiously. "And what about you? Did it feel weird to use it knowing she never did?"

Gigi shook her head. "I found a letter with my mom's will after she went missing. In it, she told me not to feel guilt over using the money and to live my life however I saw fit. Honestly, Sky, for a while I didn't use it at all because it's not like I know if she died or not. No one does. So I still see the money as hers, and I was waiting for her to come home. Then James and I got married and things changed. The trust is in both mine and my mom's names, and James somehow managed to convince me to use some of it to fund the lifestyle he desperately wanted for us. I was always hesitant, and it was a huge source of contention. But by the time I was ready to leave him, that money is what saved me. I'm just now trying to figure out what I want to do with my life besides be a reluctant trust fund baby."

He reached out a hand to her, and when she took it, he tugged her to him, giving her a quick hug. "You know there's no judgment here. I was just curious. If I were you, I'd take some of that money and start a fabulous business. Something you're passionate about and just go with it. Don't hold back. You know what I'm saying?"

"Just start a business? What kind?" she asked, amused and also intrigued by his suggestion.

"Whatever it is that gets you excited. Something to do with your herbs and potions maybe. Or go into business with me and we'll design beach wear based off of your aesthetic." His eyes sparkled with excitement. "I think I'd love to do that. Just say the word and I'm all in."

"You know, Skyler, both of those ideas are compelling, but I really don't know anything about running a business. I wouldn't know where to start." Her lack of knowledge, not to mention the overwhelming thought of running a business, was what had kept her from doing anything with her herbs and potions. It was true, she was excellent at creating skin care and healing potions, but setting up a store? That was the intimidating part.

"Start with me." He clapped his hands together and nearly jumped with excitement. "I know all about the business end. I'll teach you, or you can just help with the designing end. We'll figure it out."

"Are you serious?" she asked, frowning at him. No one just decided to go into business with someone else on a whim, did they?

"Of course I am." He gave her a frown of his own, looking affronted that she'd even asked that question. "You're my bestie. Why wouldn't I want to work with you? It's going to be a blast. Now say yes so we can check out this jewelry and then go work on a business plan."

Gigi laughed as she shook her head in disbelief. "I can't believe you just talked me into designing a clothing line with you in the span of a nanosecond. Wait until you see my design skills. Then you'll be sorry."

"Nope. Never. After a few lessons on my design software, I bet you'll be a pro. Besides, we'll do it together." He pulled her in for a fierce hug, clearly overjoyed at the decision.

"I don't know why you need me for this," she said softly. "No doubt you'd do a killer job without me, but if you're still serious when we get back to town, then I'm in."

"Oh, I'll still be serious. Now let's shop." He stepped behind the table holding the case of jewelry and said, "Help me go through this stuff."

Gigi took her spot beside him and started scanning the jewels. There were quite a few elaborate costume pieces that were made with interesting beads such as jade and jasper instead of precious gems. She helped Skyler choose a few that she thought the ladies of Premonition Pointe might find fashionable. Then they started to go through the more expensive pieces. Gigi sorted through a number of tennis bracelets, choosing one with pink diamonds and another one with alternating sapphires and diamonds.

"Those are gorgeous," Skyler said when she showed him the bracelets. "There's a ring here that goes perfectly with the sapphire one."

Gigi shifted her gaze to the ring he'd slid onto his ring finger on his right hand. As her eyes focused on the art deco diamond and sapphire ring, her heart got caught in her throat and suddenly it was hard to breathe.

"It's stunning, right?" he asked, misinterpreting her silence. "I have no idea what it will cost, but it doesn't matter. This one is coming home with me."

"Sky?" she finally forced out, her voice cracking on his name.

"Gigi? What is it? Are you okay?" He squeezed her hand, worry shining in his green eyes.

She shook her head. Gigi definitely wasn't okay. In fact, she wasn't at all sure she wasn't going to vomit. "That ring." She nodded to his hand. "Can I see it?"

"Of course." He quickly took it off and placed it in the palm of her hand.

Gigi gingerly picked it up, studying the inlayed setting. It was exactly what she'd remembered with the large diamond in the middle that was surrounded by deep blue sapphires. The design was popular enough, but the setting was what made it unique with the delicate platinum inlay that surrounded it. She'd understood it to be a one of a kind, but just in case it wasn't, she tilted the ring, looking for the inscription.

When the light hit it just right, she gasped, reading the date: 02/14/80. Her birthday.

"Gigi. You're freaking me out. What is going on?" Skyler demanded, his worried eyes searching hers.

"This ring," she croaked out as she held it up. "It's the one my mother was wearing the day she disappeared."

CHAPTER TEN

Skyler blinked at Gigi, shock written all over his face. When he finally found his voice, he asked, "How is that possible? Are you sure?"

Gigi nodded, her entire body numb. She showed him the engraved date. "That's my birthday. She got this as a gift from her mother when I was born."

"Holy shit." Skyler glanced around the room, and when his gaze landed on Candy, who was walking back into the room, he marched up to her, his fists clenched and his jaw tight. "Who owns this estate?"

"I'm sorry?" she asked, glancing up from her phone.

"Who owns this estate?" he barked again.

The woman took a step back, her eyes wide with surprise as she stammered, "The heirs prefer to keep that private. They aren't interested in a media frenzy."

Skyler let out a huff of irritation and pointed to her phone. "You better disclose that right now or else I'm going to have the police crawling all over this place in about five minutes. Think about what kind of *media frenzy* that would create."

Candy snapped out of her shocked stupor and narrowed her eyes at him in irritation. "What exactly is this about?"

"A missing persons case," Gigi said calmly, knowing if they were going to get any information out of her it would be a lot easier if they weren't threatening her. Gigi held up the ring. "My mother was wearing this ring the day she disappeared twenty-three years ago. That means it's evidence in her case."

Candy eyed the ring suspiciously. "How can you be sure it was hers? You know there are hundreds of art deco rings out there from the 20s and 30s."

"Not ones engraved with the date of my birthday." Gigi cocked an eyebrow at her. "Now, do you think you can help us, or do we need to call the authorities?" Gigi knew they should probably call someone in law enforcement about the ring, but she also knew from experience that they weren't going to be excited about dealing with a cold case when the ring could have been sold any number of times.

Chances were that the owner had gotten it at an auction somewhere and had no idea who'd owned it before. Besides, the investigators she'd dealt with in the past hadn't been very forthcoming with any information they had on the case. It was always a fight to try to learn what they knew or suspected. The more information they could get from Candy, the better off they'd be. Perhaps with Sebastian's help, they could conduct their own investigation.

"I can't imagine there's any reason to call the authorities," Candy said, quickly backpedaling. "Let me just contact my boss, and then we'll see what we can do." She eyed the ring still in Gigi's hand. "I'm sure if you have proof the ring is yours we can work something out."

"I have proof," Gigi said, slipping the ring on her ring finger where her mother had worn it all those years ago. "Plenty of it."

Candy stared at the ring on Gigi's hand for a moment, seeming to debate with herself if she was going to say something about it. But she seemed to think better of the idea and excused herself to make her phone call.

Once the woman had left the room again, Gigi's knees started to give out. It was a good thing she was standing next to an armchair, otherwise she'd have likely landed on the floor.

"Holy shit, Gigi. Are you okay?" Skyler asked, kneeling in front of her.

She shook her head. Finding the ring was more than a shock. It had brought back all those feelings of terror and loss from years ago, and now Gigi was gutted. She stared at the ring on her finger and then curled her fingers to form a fist. There was no way she was taking it off again.

"I know this must be throwing you for a loop, but maybe this means you'll finally get some answers about what happened to your mom," he said gently.

Gigi closed her eyes and sucked in a sharp breath. For years, that's all she'd ever really wanted. And while she knew he was right, there was no way she could let herself hope for that. It would be too crushing when they ultimately found out that there was no way to trace the ring back to her mother. But maybe Joy would have a vision, or the ghosts in Gigi's life might have something to say about the situation. While she wouldn't get her hopes up for answers, that didn't mean she wouldn't look for them.

Heels clattered on the marble floor just before Candy reappeared. She stood in the doorway, her body rigid when she said, "My boss says we'll need proof that you're the actual owner of the ring before we can let it go. A police report or insurance claim would do."

"I have access to a police report that states my mother was wearing the ring when she went missing," Gigi said.

Candy pursed her lips together and shook her head. "How do we know your mom didn't sell it when she skipped town?"

Pure unadulterated rage filled Gigi from head to toe and her body started to vibrate. Even though her mother had never been found, Gigi was a thousand percent certain that her mother hadn't abandoned her. There was no way. "You can't be serious," Gigi said.

"I'm sorry, but as you know that piece is very valuable. We can't just let it go without proof. Especially considering the estate has a bill of sale from a reputable auction house. If you can prove it was stolen, we'll of course abide by the law to return it. But until then, it remains in the estate's possession."

"Looks like we need to get busy calling the authorities," Skyler said, his tone full of ice as he pulled out his phone.

Knowing that road would lead nowhere fast, Gigi placed a hand on his arm and turned to Candy. "How much for me to purchase the ring?"

Candy's eyes widened then narrowed. "Why would you purchase a ring you insist already belongs to you?"

"Because, Candy," Gigi said coolly, "I haven't seen my mother's ring in twenty years, and there is no way I'm walking out of this room without it. If the estate is going to fight it, that means a whole host of red tape I'll be forced to deal with all while the ring remains in your possession. I'm not willing to go that route if I can just purchase it back and take it home today."

"If it really was your mother's, then you know it's worth a

lot," Candy said haughtily, once again sounding like a pretentious snob.

"Just tell me what the estate wants for it," Gigi said, refraining from rolling her eyes again.

Candy rattled off a ridiculous number that made Skyler scoff.

Gigi offered half, and after a little bit of haggling that included the pieces Skyler picked out for his store, they came to an agreement. Candy happily ran both Skyler and Gigi's credit cards and thanked them for coming by before escorting them out of the house.

When they were back in Skyler's SUV, he turned to Gigi and said, "After the way she treated you, I wasn't going to buy anything. But you did such a good job negotiating the prices, I couldn't resist."

"I'd have been pissed if you hadn't bought them, considering you got those pieces at a steal." Gigi forced a smile as she stared down at her hand and the ring she'd thought she'd never see again.

"I think you did the right thing," he said gently. "If you'd fought them, there's a good chance it would have been 'lost' before you had a chance to make your case."

Gigi nodded. "People don't give up five figures easily. When faced with the possibility of having to hand it back to me or selling it under the table to someone else, I know which situation was far more likely."

"But now you have the ring and the auction bill of sale showing how and when it came into the estate's possession," Skyler said, nodding his head in approval. "Now you can get that sexy lawyer to investigate it, too."

"That's what I'm hoping for." She pulled the corresponding paperwork out of the bag that held the rest of the jewelry

Skyler had purchased and scanned it. It said that the Mid-Coast Auction House had acquired the ring from one in San Francisco over ten years ago. There weren't any names on the form except for an unreadable signature from the auction house manager in the lower left corner. "Looks like he's going to have his work cut out for him."

Skyler reached over and squeezed her hand. "I don't know Sebastian well, but he seems like a decent man. I'm sure he'll do everything in his power to help you."

Gigi nodded, knowing that no truer words had ever been spoken.

CHAPTER ELEVEN

*a*s suspected, Sebastian had been more than willing to put his team to work on tracking down any information from the auction houses about the ring. Unfortunately, he'd also told her that the money she spent on it was likely lost. Since she'd agreed to purchase it, the likelihood that the estate would return her purchase price was almost zero, even if she produced the police report that proved it had belonged to her mother, and the legal fees to pursue it would likely cost more than she'd spent on the ring.

That was what Gigi had expected, and she didn't regret for a moment that she'd plunked down the cash for it. All she wanted was information about who the San Francisco auction house represented when they sold it to Mid-Coast. Any clue to help her track down her mother was welcome.

Of course, in return for all of his hard work, Gigi had offered to take Sebastian out for dinner. The invitation had led to checking out her current wardrobe and trying to decide what to wear out on a date. After spending an hour trying on everything in her closet, she'd determined that either everything had shrunk in the dryer or she'd gained a few pounds.

"The dryer. Definitely, the dryer," she muttered to herself as she yanked on her yoga pants and wrestled her way into a sports bra she hadn't worn in over a year. Once she was strapped into the torture device, she pulled a tank top on and made her way outside to her back deck with her yoga mat. Surely some yoga for strength training would help her lose five pounds before dinnertime rolled around, right?

Gigi wasn't so delusional that she expected any of her clothes to feel better after one yoga session, but it would make her feel better about whatever she ordered for dinner. After pulling up a routine on YouTube, she practiced the deep breathing and did her best to follow along with the instructor.

"This isn't too hard," she said to no one as she practiced her downward dog and stretched out her calves one at a time. In fact, it felt really good, and she vowed to make yoga a daily part of her routine.

Pleased with herself, she followed along as the instructor coached her into a forward pigeon pose. The stretch felt great, and she was confident when the coach told her to sit up and reach behind her to grab one of her bent legs. That's when everything went horribly wrong.

"Oh, son of a... holy shit!" A muscle in her back spasmed, sending pain shooting through her lower back and hip that caused her to flail, leaving her lying on her side as her back continued to spasm. Tears pricked her eyes as she tried to breathe through the pain, waiting for it to subside. Only it didn't. When she tried to roll over to push herself up, another pain shot from her lower back and down her thigh. She couldn't lift her head or her arms without her entire body tensing up.

Gigi lay on her deck, staring up at the fog that was rolling in and cursing her luck. How long would she lay there until someone found her? Presumably, two and a half hours if Sebastian was on time to pick her up. Unless... She reached out for the computer, gritting her teeth against the shooting pain. By the time she pulled the laptop toward her, she was panting and sweat slicked her brow.

Gods, she must be a mess. But if she could get Skyler or one of her coven mates to hurry over and help her up, at least she wouldn't be stranded on the porch in her too tight yoga gear when Sebastian arrived.

Since her phone was in the house, all she had was email. Who was the one who was most likely to see it right away? Skyler probably, but she remembered he'd actually flown down to LA for the day to take some meetings. That left Hope, Joy, or Grace. She wasn't sure what Grace or Hope were doing, but she knew Joy was prepping for one of those commercials she was offered. It wasn't something she was excited about, but it paid too well to pass it up. Joy wouldn't mind taking a break from practicing her lines for the blood pressure medication, would she? Gigi didn't think so.

After tapping on her email, she went to the last email chain she'd had with Joy and typed an SOS message, begging her to come help. It took less than a minute for a new email to pop up, only it wasn't from Joy, it was from Sebastian, indicating that he was on his way.

"What the hell?" Gigi scanned the message and realized she hadn't replied to Joy at all. She'd replied to Sebastian, who'd CC'd her on a message to the private investigators he'd put to work on searching for the people from her past back in Bellside. "Oh, no. Holy mother of the gods. What is wrong with me?"

Gigi quickly typed back, telling him it wasn't necessary and that she already had help on the way. It was a lie, but the last thing she wanted was for her date to see her looking like a sausage in last year's yoga clothes. Okay, who was she kidding? They were clothes from five years ago, but he didn't need to see that either.

After getting an email off to Joy asking her to hightail it over, she waited for another response from Sebastian.

Nothing.

But one came from Joy, apologizing that she was in the car on her way to the dentist and that she'd call Hope or Grace and get one of them to help.

Gigi groaned and then winced when her back complained just from the breathing.

"I'm never going to do yoga again," she said, her eyes closed and her wrist resting on her forehead.

"I can't say that I blame you." Sebastian's playful tone cut through her self-pity and made her open her eyes to see him staring down at her with an amused smile. "Are you okay?"

"No. I'm just going to die right here. After I'm gone, just throw me into the ocean and let the waves sweep me out to sea," she said, trying not to wince.

Sebastian crouched down and placed a light hand on her thigh. "What can I do to help?"

There was no moving her. Not yet. She knew that was out of the question. She needed a pain potion first. "Can you go into my office and find a potion for me? It's on the second shelf from the bottom, on the far right, and it's labeled Cherry Chamomile."

"Sure. I'll be right back." She watched him stride with ease back into her house and tried not to hate him for it. Here she was trying to get into better shape for a date she had with him, and instead she'd ended up looking like a beached turtle.

Gods, she was bad at dating.

Gigi was lying there, blinking up at the afternoon sun and wishing the earth would open up and swallow her whole when Sebastian returned with the pain potion. "Found it. But wow. That room is packed. Is that what you do most days? Work on potions?"

"Yeah. I use the herbs from my gardens." She reached for the potion and grunted as pain shot down her leg again.

"Let me help." He unscrewed the cap and kneeled down to tilt the bottle toward her lips. When the potion spilled down her cheek, he was the one to grimace. "Dammit. Sorry about that. Let me try again." He slipped his hand under her head and lifted it slightly while pouring some of the potion into her mouth.

Gigi felt like a hopeless idiot, but there was nothing to do but let him help her.

It didn't take long for the potion to start to work. Not long after she swallowed, her body started to tingle, and although the pain in her back didn't go away entirely, at least she could breathe without feeling like someone was stabbing her with an ice pick.

Sebastian tilted the bottle, offering her more, but she shook her head. "That's enough for now. Can you help me up? I think a hot shower might help."

"Sure." He recapped the potion, but instead of holding out a hand to her, he bent down and lifted her into his arms, cradling her against his chest. "Upstairs? Or is there a shower downstairs you want to use?"

"Upstairs," she croaked out. "It's a walk in... if you recall."

"Of course."

The morning after their night together, he'd joined her in the shower. The experience wasn't something she'd forget anytime soon.

Once they reached the master bathroom, Sebastian put Gigi on her feet and reached over to turn the shower on. He stared at her for a moment before asking, "Do you need help, or do you prefer some privacy?"

"Uh, I've got it from here," she said. If she'd felt sexy in any way shape or form, she might have had another answer. But she was still stuffed in her too tight yoga clothes and hadn't shaved yet. There was no way she was letting him in the shower with her.

"Got it. I'll be in the other room if you need me." He pressed a kiss to her temple and walked out, closing the door softly behind him.

"Could this day be any more embarrassing?" she asked herself while looking in the mirror. It didn't take long for those words to come back to haunt her, though. While she'd managed to shuck her tank top and yoga pants without too much trouble, removing her sports bra was an entirely different matter. Lifting her arms and tugging to get the contraption over her head had her grunting in pain. She feared she'd have to learn to wear it forever, because no way was she asking Sebastian to help her with that.

Gigi managed to get the sports bra up and over her breasts and partly over her shoulders, but then the torture device got stuck, leaving her with her arms over her head and unable to move. She tried to twist and turn to loosen the hold the bra had on her, but it was too painful and not working anyway. She felt like she was trying to get out of a straitjacket. Breathing hard, with no way to budge the fabric, there was no other choice. She was going to have to cut herself out of it.

Fine. A girl does what a girl has to do.

She grimaced as she tried to bend over so that she could reach into one of her drawers for the scissors she kept there for trimming stray threads and clothing tags. But when she took a step closer to the mirror and bent over to grab the scissors, her foot slipped out from underneath her, sending her straight to the floor. Gigi cried out as she landed with her arms still bound over her head and her back spasming in pain.

"Gigi!" Sebastian burst through the door, a look of panic on his face. When he spotted her sprawled on the floor, his panic turned to shock as he reached for the scissors and stared at them in horror. They were stained with blood and looked like they'd been used in a bad slasher movie. "What happened?"

Trying not to focus on the fact that her arms were still bound over her head, Gigi glanced down at her boobs hanging out and said, "Good goddess. Why couldn't you have just let me die instead?"

"Gigi!" He dropped to his knees and wrapped her wrist in a towel. "Don't say that! Jesus, Gigi. What the hell were you thinking? I'm always here. All you have to do is ask for help. I'll do anything you need." He pulled out his phone and started scrolling, all the while holding the towel to her arm.

"Uh, Sebastian?" she asked, completely lost. "Help for what? Getting my bra off?"

"Don't play games with me," Sebastian said, anger flashing in his gray eyes. "I will not let you self-harm. Not on my watch."

"Self-harm? What?" Gigi finally glanced up at her arm and realized she was bleeding and that was why he was holding a towel to her wrist. "Oh, no. You've got it all wrong," she rushed out. "I was going to cut my bra off because it's stuck, and when I moved closer to the mirror, I slipped on the water from the shower." She glanced behind her and gestured to the open door. He'd turned it on, and some of the spray had splashed out onto the floor. "The scissors must've got me when I fell."

His eyes narrowed as he looked her over. "And what about the comment about dying?"

She couldn't stop her humorless bark of laughter. "It was a figure of speech, you freak. Look at me. My boobs are hanging out. I have a muffin top even in my underwear, and since I haven't shaved since Friday, I'm starting to look like Bigfoot. And all of this is happening in front of you. So yeah, when I asked why the universe didn't just kill me, I was joking. Though now I'm so humiliated, I'm sure I wouldn't mind if lightning shot through the window and struck me down."

His lips curved into a tiny amused smile. "Sorry to break it to you, but there's no storm brewing tonight. I doubt lightning is on its way to help you out."

"Isn't that just my luck?" Gigi said with an exaggerated sigh.

He chuckled. "How about instead of wishing for imminent death, you let me help you out of that contraption you call a sports bra. Then after we get you showered, I can take care of that cut on your arm with some antiseptic and a bandage."

"I've had worse offers," Gigi said, resigning herself to the fact that she definitely needed help and that neither Hope nor Grace were on their way.

Sebastian shook his head, obviously amused. "How do you want to do this? Sit up while I tug this bra off?"

Gigi shook her head. "I don't think that's going to work." She tried to raise herself slightly and winced. "You should just cut if off. It's too small anyway. Just free me from the damn thing and I'll swear off bras for the foreseeable future."

He glanced down at her breasts and grinned. "Promise?"

She huffed out a laugh. "Can we get on with it? I'm getting a little cold."

"Funny. I'm getting a little warm," he teased while he grabbed the scissors and started to cut.

Footsteps pounded on the wood floors outside the bathroom. "Gigi? Are you in there? I hear the shower."

"Now she's here," Gigi said, recognizing Hope's voice.

"What was that?" Hope asked, but before Gigi could answer, the door swung open, revealing a very worried-looking witch. "Gigi? What the—oh." Her eyes locked on Sebastian and then his hands and the scissors. "Oh!" She clasped a hand over her mouth, turned bright pink and then stepped back, closing the door to give them some privacy. "Sorry! Got my wires crossed. Thought you were stuck on the porch with a back spasm. Instead, it looks like your man is about to give you some other kind of spasms. I'm out! Call me if you need me."

"Hope! Wait, it's not what you think," she called through the closed door.

"It's exactly what you think, Hope," Sebastian added. "Once I get this damned bra off her anyway."

"Sports bras should be outlawed," Hope offered. Her chuckling faded as she moved away from Gigi's door.

"Oh. Em. Gee. Could this day get any more embarrassing?" Gigi asked, feeling slightly woozy as if she'd had a little too much alcohol. Only, Gigi hadn't had anything to drink besides water and some of her potion.

Sebastian raised an eyebrow at her. "You like tempting the fates, don't you?"

"Apparently, but I've already humiliated myself in front of you. What could be worse than that?"

"There you go again," he said as he finished the last cut on her sports bra. "Maybe stop while you're ahead."

Suddenly it was easier to breathe with the sports bra gone. But she didn't know if that was because she was no longer strapped into that torture device or if she was just relieved that she no longer looked like a tragedy. Either way, she was ready for that shower.

CHAPTER TWELVE

*A*s it turned out, Sebastian didn't give Gigi any spasms in the shower. He had finished undressing her, stripped his own clothes off and joined her, where he spent twenty minutes washing her hair and body. When he was done, he gently massaged her shoulders and kneaded her back with his knuckles until her knees started to weaken.

"You're really good at taking care of people," she said as he dried her off, bandaged her wrist, and tucked her into her bed. "I'm sorry our date was ruined. No more yoga for me... ever."

He chuckled and climbed onto the bed with her. His hair was wet, and he was dressed in only his jeans, making him look like sex on a stick. If she hadn't been slightly loopy because she hadn't eaten before drinking her potion, she'd have already ended the talking portion of the evening and moved on to something a little more physical.

Or she would've if her back hadn't betrayed her. Holy hell. Was that what she had to look forward to from now on? Her body breaking down while having to have someone help her up off her bathroom floor? Maybe she needed to look into getting one of those Life Alert bracelets. Did they sell them for forty-one-year-olds? Was there an age threshold she had to meet? She hoped not, because right then, she felt many years older than her actual age.

"Something tells me you'll live to yoga again," he said with a chuckle. "I hear it's really good for you if you manage to make it through a session without throwing your back out."

"Funny," she said, her tone dry. "Real crack-up."

He winked at her, kissed her gently on the lips, and sat up, leaning against her headboard. "I have some preliminary reports on the people from your past. Are you ready to hear what my guys found?"

Gigi perked up, suddenly feeling completely sober. "Yes. Everything."

He shook his head sadly. "It's not going to take long."

"Have they all moved away?" Gigi asked, prepared to be completely disappointed.

"No. Not all of them." He pulled out his phone and started reading off a list of names. A few of them had disappeared completely, and the PIs were still tracking them down. But others were still in town, and while they remembered Carolyn, no one had anything interesting to say. "There are a couple I think we should go see and talk to in person."

"Both of us?" Gigi asked.

"Yeah. We could go and act like we're there for a visit, make it more casual instead of an interrogation. What do you think?"

"Who are we going to talk to?" she asked, curious about who he thought might have some answers.

"Liza Crane, your old neighbor, and Justin Bastille, the manager of the café. And maybe her old boss, Ricky Kamp."

"Kamp!" Gigi exclaimed. "That's right. I used to call him

Kamper when I was younger. You really think he knows something?"

Sebastian shrugged. "The PI said he seemed like he was holding something back. No real lead, just a hunch. Justin remembers her well and was really talkative. If we could get more memories out of him, he might inadvertently know something. It turns out they went out on a few dates. At least according to him anyway."

"And Liza? Does she still live next door?" Gigi smiled as she thought of the woman. She'd always been kind to Gigi and her mother.

Sebastian's smile vanished, and he ran a hand through his hair. "She does live next door, but her memory is a little iffy. Anything we get from her will be unreliable at this stage, but it might be worth checking out. She also had a lot to say about your mother. It seems as if the two were close."

"I don't know about close, but Mom did rely on her a lot." Gigi frowned. "I can't imagine Liza keeping anything from the police though. She would've told them anything she knew back then. I'm sure of it."

"Not if she was trying to protect your mother," Sebastian said gently.

Her gaze snapped back to his. "Are you implying what I think you are? That my mother really did run off and let me think the worst?"

"Whoa," he said, holding his hands up in a surrender motion. "I'm not implying anything. I don't think she left you. But if there is one thing I've learned over my years of working with PIs it's to never rule anything out. We have a much better chance of figuring out the truth if we leave all options on the table. Liza clearly loved you and your mother. I think we should talk to her and see what she says. There's a good chance she's not remembering things correctly. Or if she was covering for Carolyn, maybe she'll let something slip that will help us. All we can do is try."

Gigi chewed on her bottom lip. She hated the idea of entertaining the thought that her mother had left her intentionally. As long as she lived, Gigi would never believe that she walked away just like her father had all those years ago. But Sebastian was right. They needed to talk to Liza just to see what she had to say even if she had all the details mixed up. Besides, Gigi loved Liza. It would be great to see her again. "All right. I'll do it. When do you want to go?"

"I'm pretty much free for the next few weeks, so whenever your back is better, we can make the drive down there."

"It will just be a few days," Gigi said confidently. "My potions will fix me right up."

"Really?" he asked, sounding impressed. "If it works that well, hook me up with a bottle, will you? I can always use something on hand when I pull a muscle."

"Sure." She smiled at him, pleased he was interested. Her potions weren't something she'd shared with a lot of people yet. It would be nice to get his opinion. It hit her then that she was certain that she trusted Sebastian completely. If she was willing to share her potions with him, she was already a goner. Because that was one thing that James had never had a hand in. Her gardens and her potions. They were too important to her. She'd never been willing to let him tear her down with some biting comment, or worse, try to force her to go into production with everything. He'd have taken over and turned it into a circus.

But Sebastian... he'd never do that. It was obvious that his first and only concern was Gigi. Not what kind of money she could bring in. Holy hell, every time she thought of James, she hated him more. It was a good thing he wasn't around anymore. She'd be tempted to sucker punch him in the junk the first chance she got.

"What are you thinking about?" Sebastian asked her as he tucked a lock of hair behind her ear.

She snuggled closer and rested her head on his chest. "I was just wondering why I was so stupid back then when I let you walk out of my life."

He tilted his head down and kissed her forehead. "I have no idea, love. But promise me one thing?"

"What's that?" She stared him in the eye, ready to promise him the world.

"Don't let me walk away this time." His words were soft and low, and when she nodded her agreement, he brought his lips down on hers, sealing their deal with a kiss.

Gigi's phone beeped with a message, causing them to tear themselves away from each other. She grabbed her phone from the nightstand and burst out laughing when she read the message from Hope.

It looks like you're in for one wild night. Don't forget the whipped cream. If you need a reminder on how to make a whipped cream bikini, just let me know. Lucas and I will make a video. Wait, scratch that. We don't have any whipped cream. But we do have caramel sauce. That would be hot, right? Maybe too hot on my lady bits, but you get the picture. Have fun. Use protection. And call me the minute he leaves. I'm just dying to know what went on in that bathroom. Looked like some light BDSM. Only hotter. Later.

"Who is it from?" Sebastian asked lazily.

"Hope." She read him the message, barely able to contain her laughter.

"Caramel sauce? Is she serious?"

Gigi nodded. "No doubt about it. She's the crazy one of the group. Or maybe just the most adventurous."

"Well then. We can't let down Hope, can we? I'll grab the sauce. You be thinking of all the places you want me to lick it off of you."

Gigi laughed to herself.

"What?" he asked.

"Nothing. Nothing at all," she said, grinning at him. Only Sebastian would catch her hogtied in a sports bra and flailing all over the floor with a back spasm and still decide she was sexy enough to break out the caramel sauce.

Seriously, what had she been thinking when she let him walk away all those years ago when she'd chosen James?

There was no answering that question. All she could do was look forward, and it was starting to become very clear that she wanted Sebastian Knight to be her future.

CHAPTER THIRTEEN

"This one," Gigi said confidently as she pulled a cream-colored beaded dress off one of Skyler's racks. She handed it to Joy and said, "Go try it on."

Joy eyed the gown, her brows knit together as she studied the formfitting, sleeveless dress with the deep dip in the center that would no doubt show off all her assets. "You don't think it's too sexy?"

"Do you really want to do menopause and blood pressure commercials for the rest of your life?" Gigi asked. "Because if you show up at the gala in something covering every inch of your body, that's how they'll pigeonhole you."

"Ugh. No. If I never do one again, it will be too soon." She took the dress from Gigi and walked to the back of the boutique where the dressing rooms were.

"She's going to look hot in that," Skyler said, looking up from a stack of paperwork on the counter.

"It's perfect for her," Autumn agreed. His new assistant was stocking the store with the various vintage items he'd picked up over the last few weeks while he worked on the overall design elements and followed up with his suppliers for his new designs.

"Autumn has a really good eye. We're thinking of making her a stylist for those customers who need a little extra attention," Skyler said, beaming at her. "I swear, she's already made my life a thousand times easier."

Gigi smiled at them. Skyler really was on cloud nine, and Autumn was buzzing around like she'd been working for him for years. It was crazy how they'd hit it off so quickly. But she was happy for her friend. He'd wanted a business model that kept him closer to Premonition Pointe, and it looked like his store was going to be a hit. They weren't even opening to the general public for at least a few weeks, and already that morning he'd let three clients in to shop his stock. Carly Preston and one of her friends as well as Joy. Skyler's shop was really the only one in town with high-end clothing that catered to those who needed something more glamorous than casual beachwear. "It sounds like a match made in heaven."

"Perhaps." Skyler winked at Autumn, who was smiling to herself as she rearranged one of the racks she was working on. "But I think we need a third to really pull this all together."

"A third what?" Gigi asked, confused. "Another stylist or assistant?"

"Hopefully both, eventually, but no. That's not what I'm talking about." He tucked his hand through her arm and tugged her over to the empty space between one of the front windows and the checkout counter. "I need my partner to fill this space with her luxury skin care line and healing potions."

Gigi blinked at him. "What?"

"You heard me," he said, beaming at her. "My target market for this clothing boutique is the same one that is perfect for your beauty line or high-end potions. Wouldn't it be great to start out here, where you don't have to worry about anything but keeping us stocked?"

"But I thought you were going to fill this space with jewelry," she said, still shocked he was seriously talking about carrying her products. Products he hadn't even used.

"Oh, that's going on the other side of the checkout counter." He waved an unconcerned hand. "This space right here is reserved for you if you want it. If you don't, I can source some products from Los Angeles, but I'd really rather use local products. People really like that."

"You haven't even used my products," she said, still unable to wrap her head around this idea of his. "You can't just take my word for it that they're good."

He snorted. "Oh, honey. Of course I have. Remember that face cream you gave me a month ago? And the lip balm you tucked into my pocket that day my lips were so sun chapped that I looked like a lizard person? Don't forget about all the herbal tea you're always serving us when we're over. Remember the one for virility you made us that one day? Girl, Pete still talks about that night."

"I know. He's always asking me for more. I keep telling him he has to wait until the herbs are back in season," Gigi said with a laugh. "He has to wait until fall."

"Fall!" Skyler's eyes widened. "You can't be serious."

Gigi chuckled. "For that particular one. I'll work on something else if things are that dire."

"Bite your tongue. Our sex life is *not* dire," he insisted, looking affronted at her conclusion. "It just isn't usually that… intense."

"Oh." She placed her hand over her mouth and giggled. "I see. Well, in that case, I'll try to work on something else that might spice things up a bit."

"Good," he said, looking pleased. "Now. What about this?" He waved a hand at the empty space. "Do you want to think it over? Read a contract? Tell me to mind my own damned business? I'm ready for anything you decide. But let me just say that I think you're amazing. Your products are better than anything out there, and I'd be thrilled to partner with you if you're up for it. I know you've got other things on your mind right now, so if you don't—"

"I'll do it," Gigi said, cutting him off. "Get me a copy of the contract so I can look it over, but yes, I want to do it."

Skyler's eyes lit up. "Really?"

"Yes, really." Unadulterated joy slammed into Gigi as the idea of selling her potions really hit home. Having Skyler offer retail space without her having to figure out how to run her own store was just about the best scenario imaginable. It wasn't something she'd really allowed herself to dream about through the years, but now that it was a real possibility, she felt like she'd explode with happiness. "I'm very excited about this."

"Excited about what?" a familiar masculine voice asked from behind her.

Gigi turned to find Sebastian in jeans and a black T-shirt that did a spectacular job of showing off his shoulders and biceps. His dark hair was messy as if he'd been caught in the wind, and Gigi thought he'd never looked sexier. "Hey, you. You're early."

"Just a few minutes," he said, glancing at his phone. "You said noon, right?"

"Is it that late already?" Skyler exclaimed. "Holy shit. I've got a Zoom meeting that starts in two minutes. Gotta go." He quickly hugged Gigi and added, "I'll email you the contract. Don't be afraid to let me know if something doesn't sit right."

"Okay." Gigi hugged him tightly and whispered, "Thank you."

"No problem, sweets." He winked and rushed to his office in the back of the store.

Gigi turned to Sebastian. It had been a couple of days since she'd nearly killed herself trying to yoga, but her potions and creams had worked, and she was feeling as good as new. Sebastian was there to pick her up so they could head back to their hometown and see if they could shake any information loose from the people who still resided there. Gigi had gotten so caught up in her new business opportunity, she'd almost forgotten she was expecting Sebastian at any moment. "I guess time got away from us."

He chuckled. "Isn't that always the case when it comes to you and Skyler? Are you ready to go?"

"Just one minute. Joy is still looking for a dress. Let me tell her I'm leaving." Gigi moved back toward the dressing rooms with Sebastian following her.

"The store is looking really good," he said.

"It's gorgeous, isn't it?" Gigi glanced over her shoulder, smiling at him. "I can't wait to be a part of it."

"Oh, are you going to work for Skyler?"

"Not for, with. In fact, I have a contract I need you to look over later if you don't mind. Skyler is going to stock my potions and skin care line."

"I'd be happy to," he said. "And congratulations. It sounds like you're excited about it."

"I am." Gigi stopped when her eyes landed on Joy standing in front of a three-panel mirror, looking like a goddess in the beaded gown. "Holy shit, Joy. You look like a movie star in that dress. You have to get it."

"I was going to right up until I saw this." She bent her leg, making it peek out from a slit in the skirt that was just about waist high.

"That just makes it better. Sexy as hell. Right, Sebastian?" she asked the man behind her.

He cleared his throat. "The lady isn't wrong, Joy. I'm sure Troy would be proud to escort you to the gala in that."

"As long as you don't plan to wear see-through panties and have a wardrobe malfunction, then I don't see the issue," Gigi said, frowning at her. There was no way Gigi was letting her friend leave without that dress. It was just too perfect for her.

"Look at this!" She moved the skirt aside and pointed to her thigh. "I can't let any of those Hollywood types see my cellulite!"

Gigi squinted at her leg, trying to make out any dimples in her skin. "I'm not seeing it. And aren't you the one they wanted to use for an underwear ad? I don't think they see what you see."

"Ugh." She pulled the skirt back over her leg. "It's not terrible, but I just noticed it while I was looking in the mirror. If a photographer gets it on film, I will be mortified," Joy said, sounding a little panicked.

"Get the dress. I'll take care of the cellulite." Gigi rummaged around in her purse until she found the small jar of cream that Joy had passed on from Carly Preston. "Use this. It works. I know because I tried it a few times, and Carly is a genius. You'll be fine."

"Are you sure?" Joy asked, her face lighting up. "It really works?"

"It did for me. Smoothed my thighs right out. Since you barely have any cellulite, I think just a dab will clear it right up for you."

"Thank you." Joy tucked the little jar into her palm and reached out to hug Gigi. "I'm really glad you came to town."

Gigi chuckled. "Thanks. But I think the person you need to thank is Carly. Tell her I think it's great and if she wants me to try anything else out, I'm happy to do it."

"I will." Joy glanced at Sebastian. "I guess you two are ready to head out?"

Gigi nodded. "Yep. We'll be gone for a few days. I'll call you when we're back, and we can set up a time for the coven to meet. Sound good?"

Before Joy could respond, Gigi's phone made an unfamiliar beeping noise. Gigi pulled it out and frowned. "I don't know why it's doing that."

"It's a dating app notice," Autumn said, popping up from one of the merchandising displays. "It happens when someone messages you."

Sebastian stiffened beside Gigi, and in a tight voice, he asked, "Dating app?"

"Oh, dammit. I forgot all about that thing." Gigi turned to Sebastian. "Skyler talked me into setting it up a while ago. Even though it's called Exclusive, the matches were so bad, I logged out and never went back. Obviously, since I had no idea what the notices sounded like." She tapped on her phone and deleted the app without reading the message. "There. All gone."

"I should do that, too," Autumn said. "It's worse than picking up someone at a bar. At least when you're face-to-face you can see if there's any spark before you agree to a drink or, god forbid, dinner." She visibly shuddered. "The last date I went on, the guy took me to dinner at his mother's house because the food was free."

"No!" Gigi put a hand over her mouth to stop the laughter from bubbling up. "Tell me you're joking."

"Nope. And it gets worse. He and his mother started talking about wedding plans. I was to wear a champagne-colored dress because they were certain I wasn't a virgin, and white is only for the virginal brides. But before the wedding, they needed me to go to a fertility doctor, just to make sure my pipes are in good order so I could produce an heir or two in the first couple of years. Grandchildren were nonnegotiable. If that wasn't enough of a shit pie, she also wanted me to learn to groom her poodle because she was tired of paying money to the groomers and I had to earn my keep somehow. You know, because I'd be her daughter-in-law and wouldn't want to be cut out of the will."

Gigi stared at Autumn, unable to form words.

"I hope you got up in the middle of dinner, flipped them the double birds, and stole the dessert on the way out," Sebastian said, his tone full of outrage on her behalf.

"It was something like that. Too bad the dessert was coconut cream. I can't stand it. But I took it anyway just out of spite."

Sebastian let out a bark of laughter.

"You went through all of that and you still haven't deleted the dating app?" Gigi asked, unable to comprehend going out with anyone after a date like that.

"I'm an eternal optimist," Autumn said dramatically, placing a palm over her heart. "One day I fully expect to meet my Mr. Right."

"That *is* optimistic. Despite my reservations, I hope it does work out for you. Or you maybe try the bar option instead."

"Maybe I will," she said as she moved to begin organizing another rack. After chuckling to herself, she looked up and said, "Enjoy your trip down south."

"Thanks, Autumn," Gigi said, waving at her while pulling

Sebastian to the door. If they didn't make a break for it while everyone was busy, they'd never leave.

Once they were outside, Sebastian wrapped his arm around her shoulders, kissed her temple, and said, "I hope you have some good stories, because you do realize I'm going to want to hear all about your dating-app rejects while we travel to Bellside. That should keep us entertained for a while."

Gigi shook her head, chuckling. "You don't know what you're asking for."

"Sure I do. I want to hear the good, the bad, and the ugly."

Gigi paused just before climbing into the SUV and said, "Great. Dick pics it is then. I hope you like ugly cocks, because I've got a lot in my inbox now."

"Seriously?" he asked, looking horrified again.

She shrugged. "I guess you're about to find out."

"What have I gotten myself into?" he asked before slipping into the driver's seat.

Gigi chuckled to herself, slid into her seat, and said, "Seriously though, even if all of them hadn't been creepy or inappropriate, I don't think I actually would have gone on a date with any of them."

He looked over at her before backing out of the space. "Why?"

"Because you were back in town, and no matter how much I lied to myself, the truth was you're the only one I could think about."

A slow smile claimed his lips. "That's good, because I've been thinking about you for over twenty years. And now that I have you, I'm going to have real trouble giving you up."

Butterflies sprouted in her belly. "Just don't make me a fertility appointment or expect me to push out a few kids and I think we'll be all right."

"Deal. Can I take you to my mother's for a free meal?" he asked, smirking at her.

"You better." Gigi grinned at him. "Because I can't wait to see Shannon. It's been too long."

"That's what she said. I'll make sure she keeps the wedding attire comments to herself until next time."

Gigi snorted. "Good luck with that one."

CHAPTER FOURTEEN

"*L*ook at that ring," Shannon Knight said, practically drooling on the sapphire and diamond ring that had belonged to Gigi's mother. They were in Sebastian's childhood home with his mom, a place where Gigi had always felt safe as a kid. Their home had been her safe haven. She was suddenly glad that Sebastian had wanted to stop there first. She'd missed his mom terribly, too.

After a few moments, Shannon's head snapped up and she zeroed in on Gigi's gaze. "Did my son finally get up the nerve to ask you to marry him?"

As Gigi expected, it only took twenty-two minutes until Shannon Knight found a way to ask if she and Sebastian had plans to head to the alter. The poor woman had spent years predicting that Gigi and her son would get married on the beach at sunset and have four kids within four years. Rolling her eyes, Gigi pulled her hand from Shannon's and said, "No. This ring belonged to my mother."

Shannon placed a hand over her own heart and said, "I'm sorry, Clarity. I know you miss her terribly."

"She goes by Gigi now, Mom," Sebastian said gently, giving his mother a kiss on the cheek.

"Right. Old habits are hard to break," Shannon said with a wry smile.

"It's all right. But yes, I do miss her." Gigi said. "But that's what these next few days are about. We're going to try to gather information about the day she went missing so that I can finally get some closure. If nothing turns up, that's fine, too. I'll just have to find a way to let her go on my own terms. But today, I'm seeking answers."

Shannon squeezed Gigi's hand and said, "You let me know if there is anything I can do. If it's possible, I'll make it happen."

"Thanks, Shannon. You're the best. I can't tell you how much it means to me that you were here for me back then. I wish now that I'd have kept in touch," Gigi said, feeling ashamed of the way she'd walked away from everyone back then. Why had she let go of every relationship she'd had? "I'm sorry I stopped returning your calls. I just..." Gigi shook her head. "I was a mess."

"Oh, honey. That was such a trying time," Shannon said, pulling her into a hug. "I don't fault you for a thing. You were only trying to survive it. Everyone handles trauma differently. I just wish James hadn't isolated you so much."

"Me, too." It had taken Gigi a long time to realize that James had manipulated her into distancing herself from Shannon and Sebastian. Clearly, he'd thought them a threat. He'd been right of course. If they'd seen what she couldn't, they'd have done what they could to warn her. "But he's out of my life now, so it's time to move forward. Thank you for everything you did back then."

"You don't need to thank me," she said, pulling back and wiping at her damp eyes. "Just be happy. That's all I want."

Gigi glanced over at Sebastian, a small smile curving her lips. She'd already found her happiness when she'd dumped James and moved into her house, but having Sebastian back in her life and by her side was more than she'd ever hoped for. "I am."

"I can see that." She beamed at both of them. "Come on. Let's get your things tucked into the guestroom."

"Uh, Mom, what guestroom?" Sebastian asked. "If you're talking about my old room with that old double bed, I think Gigi and I would be more comfortable at the hotel in town."

"You will do no such thing," Shannon insisted. "It is your old room, but there's a queen in there now. I updated the furniture six months ago. If you came to visit more often, you'd know that. This way." She gestured for them to follow her.

Gigi shared a glance with Sebastian and then whispered, "She's putting us in the same room?"

Sebastian let out a bark of laughter and said, "I'm a forty-two-year-old man, Gigi. I think my mother is well aware I'm not a virgin."

"I should hope not," Shannon called over her shoulder. "Sex is excellent for overall mind and body health. Just as long as you two keep the volume down, it's all good."

Sebastian chuckled while Gigi closed her eyes, mortified.

"I am not having sex with you in your mother's house," Gigi whispered.

"Forget it, Mom. We can't stay here. Gigi won't put out if there's a chance you can hear us," Sebastian called after her.

Shannon opened a bedroom door and paused, glancing back at them. "No problem. I've got ear plugs. I won't hear a thing."

Gigi buried her face in her hands and muttered, "Oh my god. I can't believe this is happening."

Sebastian pressed his hand to the small of her back and said, "Come on. Let's check out the sex cave."

Gigi groaned. "You do know there's zero chance with me while we're here, right?"

He chuckled. "We'll see."

"I hate you," she lied. But when his hand slid up to her neck and massaged gently at the base, she felt that familiar tingle only he could coax out of her and knew that once she was wrapped in his arms, her resolve would vanish faster than a box of Krispy Kremes at a coven meeting.

Still chuckling softly, Sebastian pressed a kiss to her temple and said, "No you don't. Now, let's go check out our temporary digs."

The room was nothing like Gigi remembered. The old double bed had been replaced with a gorgeous platform bed that had a gray upholstered headboard and was made up with a fluffy white comforter and matching pillows. A soft gray throw was at the end. The distressed off-white dresser and nightstands added an interesting coastal look to the room.

"Shannon, this is really lovely. And it doesn't smell like teenage boy either," Gigi said, winking at Sebastian.

His mother laughed. "You have no idea how many room fresheners I went through after he moved out just so I could reclaim this room."

Sebastian groaned as he put their overnight bags on top of the dresser. "Can we not gang up on younger me?"

"But that's half the fun of coming to see your mother," Gigi teased.

He rolled his eyes. "Whatever. I'll leave you two to it then.

I'm going to go grab a beer and see what kind of snacks I can find."

"The more things change, the more they stay the same," Shannon said with an exaggerated sigh. "The chips are in the pantry and the onion dip is in the fridge."

"You're the best mom in the whole world," he said and disappeared down the hall.

"He's still seventeen, isn't he?" Gigi asked with a laugh.

"Some days," Shannon said with an amused smile. "But seriously, I couldn't be prouder of the man he's become."

"He's definitely the best man I know," Gigi said.

Shannon's expression turned serious as she reached for Gigi's hands and held them tightly. "I know you're here for answers about your mom, and I really hope you find them. But try not to lose sight of who's right in front of you, okay?"

Gigi glanced at the open door and cleared her throat. "I really care about your son, Shannon. If you're asking me not to hurt him, then you don't have anything to worry about there. That's the last thing I want to do."

Shannon gave her a small knowing smile. "Oh, honey. I'm not concerned about Sebastian. It's true I don't want to see him hurt, but he can handle whatever comes his way. It's you I'm worried about. Things haven't exactly gone smoothly for you since your mother disappeared, and there's nothing I'd like more than to see you truly happy. It's no secret that I hope that you'll end up with Sebastian, but if he's not the one, then he's not the one. I just want you to see there's someone who loves you completely and wants nothing but the best for you. He's the real deal, and if you let him, he'll be there for you for the rest of his life."

Tear stung Gigi's eyes, and in that moment, she didn't even bother to try to blink them back. She knew Shannon was right.

Sebastian was that kind of man. Gigi just hoped she was worthy of him. "Thank you," she whispered to Shannon. "I think I needed to hear that."

Shannon opened her arms wide, and Gigi didn't hesitate to step into them. As Shannon hugged her, Gigi rested her head on the other woman's shoulder and felt something shift inside of her. For the first time since her mother had disappeared, Gigi's anxiety about the future seemed to dissipate. Maybe it was because Shannon was a mother figure she trusted. But more likely it was because she was finally whole enough to accept Sebastian's love and everything he had to offer.

"I love you, Gigi," Shannon said. "You deserve the world."

Gigi swallowed the lump in her throat and forced out, "I love you, too. Thank you for... Just thank you."

"$\mathcal{M}$ain Street looks exactly the same," Gigi said as Sebastian parked right in front of Beach Beanies, the local café. "It's weird being back here."

"I felt like that the first time I came back here after college," Sebastian said. "It had been over three years, and it just seemed so surreal. It didn't help that I kept expecting news stories to pop up, but thankfully they never did."

Gigi reached over and grabbed his hand, her heart hurting for him. She wasn't the only one who had experienced trauma around her mother's disappearance. The entire town had blamed him just because he was the last person who'd seen her. It wasn't fair, and the accusations had sent him running from his hometown, his mother, and Gigi. "I'm sorry."

He squeezed her hand. "I know, but it wasn't your fault. Let's go inside and see if we can finally find us both some closure."

Gigi leaned over and gave him a slow kiss before finally pulling away and climbing out of the SUV. When he joined her on the sidewalk, she asked, "Do you think Justin is working tonight?"

"He should be. The PI's notes say this is the night he closes." Sebastian slipped his hand around Gigi's, and together they walked into the café. There was only one lone female customer sitting near a window. The man behind the counter was older than Gigi remembered, but he had the same wavy hair, wideset eyes, and stocky build. There was no doubt he was Justin, though he weighed a little more and his hair had turned white.

They walked up to the counter and waited patiently until he put down his rag and turned to help them.

"Hey. What can I get for you?" Justin asked while logging into his register.

"Two iced lattes. Large," Gigi said.

"Got it," he said, tapping the keys. When he glanced up to take payment, he did a double take and said, "Clarity Martin? Is that you?"

"It is," she said. "If you remember me, I'm sure you remember Sebastian, too."

Justin's gaze darted to Sebastian, and the café manager seemed to shrink back a little as he took him in. He recovered quickly though, and nodded. "Of course." Meeting Sebastian's eyes, he said, "Your mother is a regular around here."

"She does like the coffee cake." Sebastian pointed to the case. "Why don't you add one to the order and we'll bring it home to her?"

"Sure thing." Justin got to work on their order. While he was making their lattes, the other customer in the store got up and left, leaving only the three of them.

Gigi watched Justin, wondering how to bring up the subject of her mother. There was just no easy way to ask, 'Hey, Justin, what do you know about my mother's disappearance that you never told anyone in the over twenty years she's been missing?' She cleared her throat and opened her mouth to ask if he remembered the last time he saw her mom, but he started talking before she had a chance.

"It's good to see you two together again," Justin said, flashing them a genuine smile. "I never did think that James guy was good enough for you, Clarity."

"That makes two of us," Sebastian muttered.

"Why do you say that?" Gigi asked. It wasn't that she disagreed with him, she was just intensely curious about what he had to say.

"You always used to order a soy caramel latte with two shots. Every time you came in, right?" The confidence in his cocked eyebrow told her he knew he was right.

"Yes. Every day on the way to school and sometimes on the way home," she said with a chuckle. "I can't believe you remember that."

He shrugged. "I know the orders of all my regulars." His mood shifted, and there was no hiding the sadness that had washed over him. "Plus, Carolyn and I were friends, so I paid a little more attention. Anyway, James used to come in and order for both of you, but half the time he ordered you a soy vanilla latte, no extra shot. A couple of times I tried to tell him he had it wrong, but he shut me down. So if you were thinking we forgot how to make your drink, that was all James."

Gigi frowned. "James never brought me anything but a soy caramel double latte. Not that he got one for me often, but when he did, it was right. Maybe your baristas just made the correct thing?" she asked hopefully.

Justin's lips flattened into a thin line. "I know I made a couple of those. And now I'm thinking maybe those lattes weren't for you. If that's the case, he was worse than I thought."

Gigi felt like she'd been gut punched. He had to be right. The one thing James had been good at in the beginning of their relationship was his attentiveness. He always made her feel seen and appreciated. But if he was buying lattes for someone else and lying about it to Justin, then there was no doubt in her mind that he'd been seeing someone else while dating her. She didn't know why she was surprised. He'd always been a selfish prick. He'd just been better at hiding it in those early days.

"Good riddance then, right?" Gigi said.

"Right." Justin handed them their drinks and the pastry. "I'm sorry. I really did think he was just thoughtless. Even if it's over, no one ever wants to hear something like that."

"It's fine," Gigi said. "Trust me, that relationship is long over. There's nothing about him that would surprise me at this point."

Sebastian took a sip from his latte before asking, "Can I ask you a few questions about the day Carolyn went missing?"

Justin frowned. "Why?"

"Clarity has reason to believe someone from her past has information that might shed some light on what happened that day. So we're just checking with anyone who knew her to see if someone might remember a detail that slipped under the radar back then."

"I didn't have anything to do with Carolyn's disappearance," he said fiercely. "Carolyn was my friend, and I was devastated when she went missing."

"I know," Gigi said, nodding at him. "That's not why we're here. I was just thinking that any small detail might help piece together what happened that day. Really, I just want to know if you saw her that day, and if so, do you remember anything about the visit?"

His expression softened as he closed his eyes and nodded.

"I've gone over it a million times in my head. She came in that morning and got a cream cheese croissant. I remember distinctly, because she used to always get the blueberry scone. But not that day. She was in a hurry, too. Said she had a shoot to get to, but didn't say where. We were discussing dinner plans for later that week when James came in and ordered the wrong drink... again. By the time I was done questioning James on if he really wanted a vanilla latte, Carolyn had left. Later I found a note in the tip jar telling me to call her. It was written on the back of a business card for some business consultant in New York. I told the police about it, but they said he wasn't anywhere near Bellside that week. I figured she just fished it out of her pocketbook. And that's it. That might also be why I don't feel so charitable about James. He interrupted my last conversation with your mother."

Justin looked so sad, and Gigi held her arms out, inviting him into a hug. The older man didn't hesitate. He stepped out from behind the counter and wrapped his arms around her, holding on tight. "I'm so, so sorry. I wish I had helpful information."

"It's all right." She patted his back. "Thank you for talking to us. If it helps, I know my mom really liked you. She just didn't really date anyone."

He nodded and pulled back, wiping at his damp eyes. "I'm sorry. It's just been so long since I talked about her with someone who knew and loved her. It's almost like her presence is here."

Gigi had to stop herself from looking around. Because she knew she'd just be disappointed. At no point since her mother went missing had Gigi felt her presence. It was probably the reason she still had a tiny bit of hope that her mother would be found.

Sebastian placed his free hand on Gigi's shoulder and said, "Justin, thank you for your time. You've been very kind and helpful. I need to get Clarity home, but have a good night, okay?"

"I will, and you do the same," Justin said, trying to sound upbeat, but his eyes were too sad. "Thanks for stopping by. It was nice to see you both."

Gigi waved and let Sebastian guide her out of the café. When they were back in the SUV, she dropped her head back against the seat and said, "That was useless."

Sebastian didn't say anything as he started the car and pulled out into the street.

Gigi waited for a few moments, but when he didn't reply, she asked, "You don't agree?"

He shrugged one shoulder. "On the surface it doesn't seem like anything to go on, but I really would love to know who those drinks were for that James was ordering."

"He probably was cheating on me," Gigi said, waving an unconcerned hand. "It wouldn't have been the only time."

Sebastian turned to stare at her. "You're not joking, are you?"

She shook her head. "I found out about a couple of his girlfriends when we were going through the divorce. It's the reason he didn't get more money in our settlement. My lawyer might have insinuated that their identities had a way of becoming public if we went to court. One of his girlfriends is the wife of one of his employers. She's also a high-profile celebrity, so that story would be in the headlines for months. If that ever came out, the partners at James's advertising firm would bury him. Since that was his worst fear, I was able to settle the divorce quickly and for a lot cheaper than I expected. He could've taken me to court and made it much more painful, but I guess his reputation means more to him than my bank account."

"Jesus, Gigi," Sebastian growled. "The more I learn about that jackass, the more I really want to kick his ass."

"Then it's a good thing I already did that, huh?" She smiled at him, feeling warm inside at having him in her corner again.

He reached for her hand and brought it up to kiss her knuckles. "It's a damned good thing, and I'm so proud of you for kicking that loser to the curb."

"Me, too. Now let's go back to your house and try out that new bed," she said, laughing.

"Don't think I won't try to get you naked," he said with a wicked smile. "We'll just pretend we're teenagers and let our hormones overrule our common sense."

Amused, Gigi said, "Since we never got to do that back then, obviously we have a lot of time to make up for."

"It's on." Sebastian pressed his foot on the gas, rushing to get them home.

CHAPTER SIXTEEN

"Good morning!" Shannon called as Gigi walked into the kitchen the next morning. "Sit down. Breakfast is already on the table."

"Smells delicious, Mom," Sebastian said from behind Gigi. "But you know you didn't need to do all this work for us. I'd have made us something."

"After that workout you got last night?" Shannon asked. "No way. You need to replenish your strength."

Gigi's face flushed so hot she was certain she was going to combust. She really had tried to be as quiet as possible the night before, because although she really hadn't intended on getting busy with Sebastian in his mother's house, she just wasn't that strong. Sharing a bed with him meant she hadn't been able to keep her hands to herself.

Sebastian laughed. "Oh, come on, Mom. You didn't hear anything. You're just fishing for information."

"Oh? Are you sure?" Shannon turned around, holding the coffee pot in one hand and the creamer in the other. "Wanna take bets?"

"Stop," Gigi said, letting out an awkward laugh. "Maybe we shouldn't talk about this."

Shannon chuckled and started filling the coffee mugs on the table.

"Mom's just joking. Aren't you, Mom?" Sebastian gave his mother a pointed look.

"Yes, I'm joking. I had that room soundproofed. You two could've been up all night swing dancing for all I'd know."

"Swing dancing?" Gigi echoed.

Sebastian rolled his eyes and grabbed the plate of waffles. "Gigi? Want one?"

"Yes." She lifted her plate out to him. After doctoring her waffle and coffee, she was grateful to have something other than Sebastian's mother to focus on.

Shannon sat next to her and patted her hand. "I'm just teasing. I didn't really have the room soundproofed."

Gigi choked on a bite of waffle. When her airway cleared, she said, "I think the next time we visit, we're gonna have to stay in a hotel."

"There's gonna be a next time?" Shannon asked, her eyes sparkling with happiness.

"Um, maybe?" Gigi said, making eyes at Sebastian, willing him to take over the conversation.

"Mother, you're about to mess this up for me. How about you stop teasing my girlfriend so she doesn't dump me before we really get started."

Girlfriend? Gigi thought. Was that what she was? They hadn't discussed it, but if she was honest with herself, she had to admit she liked the idea. She'd be pretty pissed if Sebastian went out with someone else.

Shannon's smile seemed to widen, something Gigi hadn't really thought was possible. "I'm sorry, Gigi. I didn't mean to make you uncomfortable. I might've had a score to settle with my son."

"Oh, this again?" Sebastian said, laughing. "It's not my fault you and Blake act like you're training for the Olympics in the bedroom. All I said was that you might want to try to keep it down when your son is home."

Gigi ate in silence as she listened to the easy banter between Sebastian and Shannon. Even though Shannon's teasing had made her uncomfortable, she enjoyed watching them together. Sure they were mother and son, but there was a close friendship between them, too. It was a special bond she found herself envying. She imagined that this was the type of relationship that she'd have had with her own mother if she'd been given the chance.

"Will you two be back for dinner tonight?" Shannon asked.

"Yes, but we're taking care of it tonight," Gigi said. "Sebastian said your favorite dish is lasagna, so I thought I'd make us a batch as a thank you for your hospitality."

"You really don't have to, Gigi. I don't mind—"

"I want to," she said, squeezing Shannon's hand. "Just maybe no more talk about bedroom antics? I like it here, so I'd hate to have to insist on a hotel room the next time we come visit."

"Hear that, Sebastian?" she asked her son reverently. "She said next time. I promise, no more teasing you about stuff I never even heard." She held her fingers up in a scout's honor symbol. "But I am gonna hold you both to that promise. Or else you can expect to see me in Premonition Pointe sooner rather than later."

Gigi laughed. "Don't worry, we'll set a date before we leave," Gigi said, making Sebastian groan.

Shannon swatted him on the arm and then gave Gigi her undivided attention as she asked about what she did for work.

And Gigi was all too happy to talk about her upcoming business venture with Skyler.

It was the best brunch Gigi had ever participated in.

* * *

LIZA CRANE'S house looked exactly as it had over twenty years ago when Gigi had left town with James. The only things that had changed were that the front porch railing was no longer broken and someone had painted the front door red, Liza's favorite color.

"Who do you think did this?" Gigi asked.

"Does she have any children?" Sebastian asked as he glanced around.

"I think so. One of each, but they don't live here. Or they didn't back then." She noticed Sebastian staring at the house next door and winced. Gigi had consciously not paid it any attention as it was too painful to relive those memories.

"Gigi, look." He nodded toward the house.

"I can't," she said, barely able to breathe.

"Damn," he whispered and pulled her into his arms. "I'm sorry, babe. I should've realized. I just wanted you to see the flowers growing along the front of the house. It looks like they're the same kind your mother had there."

Gigi couldn't stop herself. Her eyes darted to the landscaping, making her gasp a little. The flowers *were* the same. Her mother's favorites. Sunflowers, lavender, daisies, and a variety of other things that they'd planted together. But surely these were new plants. They had to be, right?

The front door of Liza's house swung open, and Liza stepped out onto the porch. Her shoulders were slightly curved in on herself and her hair was a mass of wiry gray, but other than that, she looked exactly the same as she did the day Gigi left town.

"Clarity Martin? Is that you?" Liza asked while squinting at her.

"It is, Liza. Sebastian and I just came for a visit. Is this a good time?" Gigi asked her.

"A good time?" the older woman exclaimed. "When isn't it a good time? Come in." She reached out a wrinkled hand and grabbed Gigi's, tugging her closer. Then she wrapped her small arms around Gigi and hugged the ever-loving daylights out of her. "I thought I'd never see you again, my sweet girl. Thank you for coming back."

Gigi stood there in shock as the woman held on for dear life. She and her mother had been friends with Liza, and Gigi had loved her as a child, but she'd had no idea the woman had missed her that much. If she'd known, she'd have made an effort to come see her sooner.

"It's really good to see you, Liza," Gigi said into her curly gray hair as she hugged the older woman back. "I missed you."

Liza let out a sound that resembled a choked sob, but when she finally let go of Gigi, her eyes were clear without a single tear in sight. There was joy in her dark eyes and a smile claiming her thin lips. "Come inside. We'll have tea."

Sebastian followed them into the tidy house, and when Liza instructed them to sit on the loveseat in her living room, they did as they were told.

"I'll be right back," she said, shuffling into her kitchen. When she reemerged a few minutes later, she had a lemonade pitcher on a tray and three saucers, but no cups or glasses. She frowned down at her tray and then scowled. "How are we going to eat scones, if I didn't even bring them with me?"

Gigi stood. "Let me go get them. Why don't you sit down and talk to Sebastian for a minute? Get reacquainted."

When Liza turned to him and introduced herself for a second time, Gigi's heart sank. The woman had known who she was, but there were a lot of incidents of forgetting stuff already. It was a bummer for their investigation, but more than that, Gigi was worried about her and needed to find out if anyone was watching over her.

After grabbing three glasses and conducting a futile search for scones, she settled on a package of cookies and returned to the living room, where Sebastian was telling her all about Gigi's house in Premonition Pointe.

Gigi grinned at them, filled the glasses with lemonade, and then passed out the cookies.

"Oh, these are my favorite," Liza said. "How did you know?"

"Lucky guess," Gigi said and sat next to her.

It didn't take long for Liza to start talking about Carolyn. She repeated a bunch of photoshoot stories that Carolyn must've told her years ago as if they were current. Gigi had heard all of them a hundred times before. It sort of unnerved her that Liza thought her mother was just on assignment, but she didn't bother to correct her. Why would she? Liza didn't need to relive the pain of her mother's disappearance.

Sebastian was a good sport and asked her all kinds of questions to keep Liza going. That seemed like a good plan until Liza suddenly started talking about Gigi's father.

Gigi stiffened, a reaction she always had when someone brought up her sperm donor.

"You know, I really do think your dad might be back to stay this time," Liza said, beaming at her.

"Back to stay?" Gigi forced out through the tightness in her chest. "What do you mean?" As far as Gigi knew, her father had never lived in Bellside, nor had he ever visited her.

"He was here to talk to her. Seemed real interested in a reconciliation, but you know Carolyn. She threw him out. I suppose she wants to make him work for it." Liza glanced around the room. "Have you seen my cigarettes?"

"You're smoking again?" Gigi asked, just so she wouldn't have to process what Liza had said about her father.

"I never stopped," Liza said, reaching into an oversize pocket in her sweater and producing a pack of menthol lights.

Gigi knew that wasn't correct either. She'd lived next door when Liza had suddenly quit, and when Gigi left town, it had been six months since Liza's last cigarette.

Liza lit up one of her cigarettes and then sat there and smoked it like it was the most precious thing she'd ever tasted. Maybe it was. Gigi wouldn't know, having never taken up smoking.

"Liza," Gigi said.

"Yes, dear?" She took another long drag of the cigarette and started coughing before she blew it out.

"Easy," Gigi soothed. "It's probably better if you savor it for a while."

"You're right," Liza agreed. "I wish I had one of those cigarette holders they used in the movies. Not only would I look *hot*, but I'd be the talk of the town with my tradition."

"I'm sure you would," Gigi said. "But while we're just hanging out here, can you tell me if you remember seeing or talking to my mother the day she went missing?"

Liza's eyes snapped back to Gigi's and for the first time since Gigi had arrived, she seemed so incredibly alert. "I did see her. She even came over and talked to me about... something. I have no idea what it was now. We also talked about what would happen when you went away to college. She was so proud of you."

"Thank you for saying that," Gigi said, her heart swelling because she knew without a doubt that Liza was alert in that moment.

"So was your father, you know," Liza continued.

Gigi stilled and frowned at her. "My father?"

"Yeah. Your dad. He was here that day, too. He wanted to see you." Liza picked up the glass in front of her and took a long sip.

"How could my father have been here? And why did he finally want to meet me that day?" Gigi demanded, her head spinning with the information. Her father had been looking for her? Why?

"He wanted to take you Back East so you could meet your sister," Liza said, smiling brightly.

"Sister?" Gigi asked, her voice faint now.

"Who has a sister?" Liza asked, looking around until her gaze landed on Gigi again. "Are you the sister?"

"No, I'm not *the sister*," Gigi said, disheartened and anxious. Had anything Liza said been true, or was it all just ramblings of an older woman who was slipping in and out of reality?

A knock sounded on the door, and a young man walked in without waiting for an answer. He did a double-take when he saw Gigi and Sebastian. "Who are you?" he demanded.

Gigi stood up and raised her arms in a surrender motion. "Just some old friends. I'm Clarity, and I used to live next door when I was growing up. We just wanted to say hello to Liza while we're in town. It's been many years since we've seen each other."

"Leave them alone, son," Liza chastised. "They're old friends."

"Oh, good," he said, looking relieved and squeezing Liza's shoulder lightly. "There's been some trouble of late with scammers trying to rip off older people. I'm glad you're not among them."

"Gods no," Gigi said, feeling attacked. "Truly, I just wanted to say hello. But we should go now." She gave Liza another hug and promised to visit when they were back in town again. Then she followed the young man out onto the porch. "I'm sorry we just barged in," she told him. "I didn't realize she..." Gigi trailed off, not wanting to say the words. "I'm sorry," she said again. "Liza was like a grandmother to me back when I was growing up."

"It's okay," he said. "It's good for her to have visitors. I was next door working on the flooring. I'm doing work on the house for the tenant, otherwise I would've been here to help navigate the conversation."

"You didn't need to," she said, smiling at him. He was a sweet kid, and she was glad Liza had someone like him in her corner. "Are you also the one who keeps this place up?"

He nodded. "And the one next door. Liza bought it a few years back. My father lives there now." Holding out his hand, he added, "I'm Heath, Liza's grandson and caregiver."

Gigi shook his hand. "I know it's not my place, but thank you for caring for her. I really loved her as a child. She's just the best of the best to everyone."

Heath chuckled. "All that's true, except maybe when it comes to my father. They don't really get along even though they live next to each other now." He shook his head in exasperation. "It's a weird situation, but one day he just showed up out of the blue, determined to be back in my life. It was rocky at first, but now I'm glad to get to know him." He let out a shaky laugh. "I don't know why I told you all that. I guess I just needed to get it off my chest."

Gigi nodded. "I can relate. Don't worry about it. We all need an ear every now and then. I hope it helped."

"You seem like a good person. Thank you for making her day," he said. "Come back anytime."

Gigi nodded and said her goodbyes, and when she and Sebastian were safely back in the SUV, she let out a curse. "I hate what's happened to her. Did you hear her talking about my father? I was starting to believe there was something there to pursue, but it turns out she was just confusing me with Heath," she told Sebastian. "On the one hand, I don't ever want to see or talk to my father, so that's a relief, but I hate that she's so confused."

"I know." He reached over and covered her hand with his. "I'm sorry. I know you loved her."

"I did." Gigi nodded, a tear rolling down her cheek as she left her childhood home for the last time. There would be no coming back there. It was just too painful.

CHAPTER SEVENTEEN

*A*fter taking a walk on the beach the next morning, Gigi and Sebastian stopped at Beach Beanies for lattes and then walked the short block to the office of *Central Coast Secrets*. The redheaded receptionist was a complete cliché, filing her nails and popping her gum while she stared out the window in apparent boredom.

"Uh, hello," Gigi said, interrupting her daydreaming. "I'm looking for Ricky Kamp. He's expecting me."

The receptionist pulled her gaze from the window and looked Gigi up and down. Her nose wrinkled as she said, "At least you're older than the last one."

"Excuse me?" Gigi asked at the same time that Sebastian placed his hand on her lower back.

The woman's gaze darted to Sebastian, and suddenly she sat up and pushed her breasts out. "Well, hello there, handsome. What can I help you with today?"

Seriously? Gigi thought. The woman hadn't noticed Sebastian until just that moment? If that was the case, she really was a terrible receptionist.

"I'm with Gigi," Sebastian said, giving her a cool stare.

She didn't seem to notice his social cues, or maybe she just didn't care, because without missing a beat, she grabbed a business card, wrote her number on the back and handed it to him. "You're one fine piece of manmeat. When you're done with this one, call me. I'll show you what you've been missing."

Sebastian glanced at the card, placed it back on her desk, and said, "Thanks, but I'm not interested."

The receptionist shrugged one shoulder. "Doesn't hurt to try."

"Bobbie!" a man barked from the office behind her. "Stop torturing those two. Send them in."

Bobbie rolled her pale blue eyes and waved toward the office. "I hope you have your credit cards ready. He's relentless."

Gigi ignored her comment, assuming she thought they were there to purchase advertising. When she walked into the office, she was surprised to see a man she barely recognized. Ricky Kamp had been a clean-cut businessman who always wore a suit. The man sitting behind the desk was wearing a short-sleeved button-down shirt and cargo shorts. But the real shock was his shoulder-length hair that made him look like some sort of aging hippie.

"Ricky?" Gigi said, unsure if she even had the right person.

"Clarity!" He stood and held his hand out to her.

"Hi." She shook his hand and added, "This is Sebastian Knight. He's originally from Bellside, too."

A flicker of recognition flashed in Ricky's eyes as he shook Sebastian's hand and said hello, but to Gigi's relief, he didn't bring up the accusations against him all those years ago. "It's been a real long time. How are you?"

"I'm doing well. How are you?"

"Terrific. The magazine isn't what it used to be, but I started consulting for All About Hair Tonics and now I've got extra time, extra cash, and a beach condo. I don't know what you're doing for a living these days, but I do know everyone can use extra cash." He passed a folder over to her. "Give me five minutes, and you'll be on your way to financial freedom."

Gigi blinked at him, taken aback at the sudden pitch of something that looked an awful lot like a multilevel-marketing company. "Um, I don't think this is something I'm interested in."

"It's the perfect side hustle for just about anyone," he powered on. "Within two years I began to make over six figures and as a bonus, my hair has never looked better."

That was debatable, but Gigi kept her thoughts to herself.

"Here, Sebastian, you look like a man with a good head on his shoulders. You might not need the hair tonic yet, but with that full head of hair you've got, you'd be a walking advertisement for the signature product. You should get in on this. You'd make a killing."

"I'm good," Sebastian said.

"You'd be even better if—"

"Ricky, we're actually here to talk to you about my mother. I know it's been a long time, but I'd really like to know what you remember about that day when she disappeared."

He frowned. "Your mother? I thought her case was closed."

"Not closed, just shelved. It's a cold case, but Sebastian and I are hoping to make it active again. I just need a little information. Did you talk to her that day?"

Ricky's expression turned blank as he said, "That was a long time ago, Clarity. I'm sure I disclosed any and all interactions with your mother to the police."

"I know, I just—"

"You should really try All About Hair Tonic's all-natural hair remover. It would really help with that dark stubble on your legs," Ricky said. He turned his attention to Sebastian. "I swear some people seem to just have Yeti genes. It's not their fault they have hyperactive genetics."

Sebastian coughed and muttered something about a jackass under his breath.

Yeti? What the hell was wrong with this man? Gigi glanced down. She was wearing a skirt that came just above her knees, and her legs were as smooth as could be thanks to her own special blend of hair removing cream. "I think I'll pass, but thanks for the tip."

"Your loss." Ricky moved to stand next to the window. "Your mother was a good photographer. I was sorry about what happened to her, but I can't help you. She wasn't on assignment that day. I think she might have dropped some photos off the day before, but that's all I have for you."

"She wasn't?" Gigi asked. "Are you sure?"

Ricky stared out the window and ran a hand through his hair as if he were contemplating something. Finally he turned and said, "I didn't have anything for her that day."

"But—" Gigi started.

"You can check with the police report if you don't believe me. I told them everything I knew when they interviewed me."

Gigi glanced at Sebastian. He shook his head, and she took that to mean he didn't think they were going to get anywhere with Ricky. She let out a sigh and said, "Thanks for your time. We should be going now. It's a long drive back to Premonition Pointe."

"Premonition Pointe?" he asked, his interest perking up. "All About Hair Tonic could really use consultants in that area. With the higher-end clientele there, you two could really climb the consultant ladder quickly. Especially if you tap your friends. That's where the real money is when you start to build your team."

The man was practically salivating, and it took all of Gigi's energy to smile and politely turn him down for what must have been the fifth time. No wonder he was making six figures with his hair tonics for the desperate. The man was relentless. People probably said yes just to get him to shut up.

When they were outside, Gigi said, "What did you make of that mention of my mom not being on assignment? Justin said she was on her way to a shoot. Do you think he was lying?"

Sebastian pressed his lips together. "It's hard to say. I got the impression he was holding something back, but there's no way to know what. Is it possible she was doing something independent of the magazine?"

"Maybe. She did take on private clients every now and then, but there was no evidence of that. Nothing on her calendar." Gigi let out a sigh. "Maybe Justin was mis-remembering."

"It's possible. It's been a long time." Sebastian pulled her into a side-hug. When he let her go, he asked, "Was Ricky always such a sleaze? I can't even imagine your mom working for someone like that."

"No," Gigi said. "He was a real managing editor and complete professional from what I remember. Now he's a walking infomercial. It's really disturbing."

Sebastian laughed. "You're right. That's exactly what he is. That must get exhausting."

"Can you imagine me constantly trying to pressure Grace, Hope, and Joy into becoming consultants? Or saying they had Yeti DNA?" She shuddered. "They'd probably curse me into another dimension."

Sebastian laughed and as they walked back to his SUV, they

talked about all the jobs they'd rather do than be a consultant for All About Hair Tonics. Sebastian thought for a moment. "Garbage man."

"You know, you'd make a great garbage man. And think of the workout you'd get. Maybe Troy could hook you up to model as a side job," Gigi teased, referring to Joy's boyfriend who worked in the business.

Sebastian snorted. "Maybe. Your turn. What job would you do?"

"Factory job at a cannery. Fish oils are really good for overall health," she said with a straight face.

"Bull semen collector," Sebastian said. "I read somewhere that farmers make fifty bucks for each sample."

Gigi laughed so hard she was having trouble breathing. "I know they have equipment for that, but now all I can picture is you jacking-off a bull."

He joined her in her laughter, and by the time they reached his SUV, they both had hysterical tears running down their faces.

"Come on," Sebastian said as he opened her door for her. "Let's get out of this town before you find yourself slathered in something designed to neutralize your Yeti DNA."

"Stop," Gigi gasped out. "My abs hurt from too much laughing."

Still chuckling, Sebastian picked Gigi up and deposited her into the passenger seat. "Just think of it as a good workout." He leaned in and kissed her.

It started innocently, with both of them still chuckling, but it didn't take long for Gigi to twist sideways and wrap her arms and legs around him, pulling him close. She deepened the kiss, loving the way his hard body felt against hers. She didn't know how long they stayed lip-locked, but when Sebastian finally pulled away, his face was flushed and his eyes were full of desire.

"I think we should get on the road," Sebastian said, his voice husky.

"The sooner we get back to Premonition Pointe, the sooner we can pick up where we left off," she said, brushing his dark hair out of his eyes.

He groaned. "It's gonna be one hell of a long drive today."

Gigi didn't disagree.

Once they were on the road, both of them were silent, seemingly lost on their own thoughts. Eventually Sebastian looked over at her and said, "I'm sorry the trip wasn't more productive."

Gigi glanced over at him. "It's all right. We always knew this was a longshot. I did really enjoy seeing your mom, even if she did get a little inappropriate with her teasing."

"She loved seeing you, and she didn't mean to embarrass you. That was all directed toward me. You know that, right?"

"I do. And it was funny. If I hadn't been the one sharing your bed, I'd have probably joined her. You're fun to hassle," she said, watching the way his lips twitched in amusement. Gigi could not get over just how easy he was to talk to. Their relationship back when they were teenagers had been filled with that tension of *will they or won't they*. And even though they'd been best friends, they'd each held back more than they did now, probably because of their own insecurities and lack of maturity. But now? She felt like she could say anything to him and it would be fine. She'd never had that with anyone before. Ever.

"Sebastian?" she said.

"Yeah?"

"Are we dating now?" She hadn't missed it when he'd called

her his girlfriend, but they hadn't actually discussed making anything official.

"If you're not sure, then I think I'm doing it wrong," he said teasingly.

She rolled her eyes at him. "Obviously we're doing something. Dating, sleeping together, I don't really know what we're calling it."

"We're calling it a relationship," Sebastian said, all traces of amusement gone. "I want you, Gigi. I think I've made that fairly clear."

"So we're exclusive?" she asked.

"Damn right we're exclusive, and the next time I introduce you to someone, it's going to be as my girlfriend. Are you good with that?"

Gigi grinned at him. "Yes."

He glanced over at her, his gaze boring into hers for just a moment. Then his tone softened, and he reached for her hand, taking it in his. "It's about time, Gigi. After you kept pushing me away when I got to town, I was really worried you'd make me wait another twenty years."

"To be honest, Sebastian, I was worried, too. But you're far too irresistible, and now you're stuck with me."

"Thank the gods for that."

CHAPTER EIGHTEEN

*G*igi's investigation into her mother's disappearance had stalled. Sebastian was currently up in San Francisco, trying to trace the bill of sale on the ring, but other than that they'd exhausted all the avenues they could think of to find someone from Gigi's past who had knowledge of her mother's disappearance. Having only a cryptic message from a ghost wasn't enough for her to keep torturing herself. If she had any solid leads, she'd go to the ends of the earth to find out what happened that day, but as things stood, it was just too painful.

Instead, she was focusing on her skin care line that she was debuting at Skyler's shop. The soft opening was being held in just over two weeks. That meant she was spending a lot of time with her herbs, producing enough inventory to stock the shelves. It was a lot of work, but she'd never been happier.

Sebastian had vetted the contract Skyler had given her and said it was more than fair, and in his opinion, overly generous for their type of arrangement. Gigi hadn't hesitated to sign it, and that day Skyler had helped her design the labels to go on her products. They were gorgeous and branded with a small cluster of sunflowers. Gigi couldn't have asked for anything more beautiful.

As soon as Gigi had signed the contract to work with Skyler, she'd turned one of her garage stalls into a studio and had gotten to work. It was a sort of haven for her, where she lost herself in the work and felt really good after a day of being productive. It was the first time in her life that she had something meaningful to do with her days, and it turned out that she adored her new reality.

About a week after she'd gotten back from Bellside with Sebastian, she was in her studio working on a sunscreen when she realized she was going to run out of packaging if she didn't order more as soon as possible. After washing her hands, she went inside and sat at her kitchen bar drinking a cup of tea as she stocked up on supplies.

Gigi was just about to close her laptop when a new email came in from Exclusive, the dating app she'd deleted off her phone. The message headline read: *You have a new message from Lawman0208.*

Her immediate instinct was the delete the message. But then she looked closer at the username. *Lawman0208.* Sebastian's birthday was the eighth of February, and he was an attorney. Was he messaging her through the dating app?

She frowned. Why would he do that? There was no way she could ignore the message. She had to know if it was him, and if it was, why he was messaging her. After grabbing her phone and reinstalling the app, she clicked on the message and grinned. The profile picture and message confirmed it was indeed her boyfriend.

Lawman0208: *Hey gorgeous. I know you deleted the app, but it looks like you need help disabling your profile. If you get this message, hit me up and I'll trade you a midnight stroll on the beach for help figuring out how to dump this hellscape dating service.*

Herblover: *You've caught me. Technology isn't my strong suit. I think I was born a decade too early. You know I love midnight strolls on the beach. Where and when?*

Gigi started to put her phone down, but Sebastian messaged back instantly, making her heart flutter with anticipation.

Lawman0208: *Is tonight too soon?*

Herblover: *Tonight? Aren't you out of town? I thought you weren't going to be back until tomorrow.*

Lawman0208: *Right. Just wishful thinking, I guess. Tomorrow then?*

Herblover: *Perfect. Tomorrow. Midnight. Crescent Beach?*

Lawman0208: *I'll be the one with the hard cider and apple turnovers.*

The green light that had been next to his name disappeared, making Gigi assume he'd logged out. She kept staring at that last line. Hard cider and apple turnovers. At one time in her life, she'd been obsessed with both. But she was pretty sure that had been after he'd left Bellside. Or was it? Her memory of that time was pretty spotty.

Chuckling at herself, she got off the chair and practically skipped back to her studio. Sebastian had just scored major points. He'd remembered two things: That she loved walks on the beach at midnight. She'd always thought that time of night was magical. That had been enough to impress her on its own, but then he'd gone and remembered that she used to love cider and apple turnovers. Had James ever paid any attention to what she wanted? She scoffed. No. He hadn't. Not really. And definitely not when it counted.

The memory of James instantly put her in a foul mood, and

she mentally berated herself for comparing the two men. She had to stop thinking about her ex every time Sebastian did something to please her. She should be thinking about Sebastian and just how incredible he was.

"Get it together, Gigi," she told herself. "James is long gone. There's no reason to even be thinking about him anymore." The words came easily. It was just a matter of making her brain cooperate. It wasn't easy, but she was working on it.

* * *

"WHERE'S SEBASTIAN TONIGHT?" Joy asked as she slid into the chair next to Gigi. They were at Blueberries, a farm-to-table restaurant in town, and still waiting for the famous actress Carly Preston to join them. When Gigi had first gotten the invitation to have dinner with Joy, she hadn't really been in the mood to socialize, but Joy talked her into it by letting her know that Carly really wanted to talk shop about Gigi's new skin care line. Carly had been gifted samples, and Gigi was intensely curious about what she had to say about her products.

So instead of staying curled up on her couch, she'd dressed up, curled her hair, and painted on her favorite red lipstick. When she'd checked herself out in the mirror, she'd barely recognized the woman staring back at her. She was well rested, happy, and looked like a million bucks, thanks to the skin care products she'd recently refined for women of a certain age.

"Sebastian's in San Francisco working on tracing the history of the sale of my mother's ring," Gigi told Joy as she held her hand out, admiring the gorgeous piece of jewelry. "He thinks that if he can find the authentication papers, we might be able to trace who brought it to them before they auctioned it off."

"Wow. That would really be a breakthrough, wouldn't it?" Joy opened her menu, scanned it briefly, and then closed it again. She turned her attention to Gigi and raised an eyebrow, clearly still waiting for an answer.

"Yes. It really would," Gigi said quietly, still staring at the ring. Sadness washed over her, and Gigi wondered if there was ever going to be a day when the pain from the loss of her mother didn't feel like it was going to shatter her heart.

Joy reached over and covered Gigi's hand. She didn't say anything; she just squeezed, silently offering her support.

"Thank you," Gigi whispered. "You're a really good friend."

"So are you." Joy leaned into her, making their shoulders bump before she straightened and flashed a smile at the gorgeous green-eyed blonde that had lit up movie screens for the past forty years. "Carly," Joy said, standing and holding her arms out to the other woman. They hugged, and when Joy pulled back, she scanned Carly and nodded her approval. "You look incredible. Love this off-the-shoulder number, and those skinny jeans do fabulous things to your back side."

Carly flushed slightly, and Gigi knew in that moment what everyone loved about the actress. Sure, she was great at her job, but there was something so charmingly wholesome about her that it made it difficult not to instantly love her. "Thanks," Carly said to Joy as she leaned in and gave her an air kiss. "You're not looking too bad yourself. Love that dress."

"It was a gift from Troy. He said he wants to do a shoot in the woods. Isn't this perfect?" She twirled and showed off her fairy-like flowy dress that was covered in flowers and butterflies.

"It's gorgeous on you," Gigi said. "You have the perfect willowy body for that type of dress."

Carly nodded her agreement, and then both women turned their attention to Gigi. "Joy's not the only one who looks camera ready," Carly said to her. "My goodness woman, you look absolutely radiant."

"Radiant?" Gigi asked. "I think you two might need your eyes checked. When's the last time you got your contact prescriptions updated?"

"I actually got mine checked about a month ago," Carly said, laughing. "But I like your style. Kinda funny, even if you were hitting below the belt with the old-age eyesight jokes. Just you wait. One of these days, you'll wake up and squint because you can't see across the room. Then when you look at your phone, you can't see that either. Literally, you'll be flying blind until you can get your appointment. Which will be about two to three weeks, because everyone else you know in your age group is going blind, too."

Joy just shook her head. "I'm not stepping into this one. But, Gigi, we weren't kidding. You're glowing. If that's the new skincare line and not a surprise pregnancy, then I'm gonna be first in line at Skyler's boutique opening. Cause damn, girl, you look hot."

"Surprise pregnancy? Bite your tongue. That's the last thing I need right now," Gigi said.

"I notice you didn't deny that it might be a possibility," Joy teased. "Does this mean things with Sebastian have heated up?"

Oh hell, Gigi thought. She wasn't one for sharing her personal life. She'd never been a part of a close circle of friends whom she could talk to, and now she just felt weird about it. "Um... pretty sure there's no surprise baby."

Carly grimaced. "That means there could be, right?"

"I guess, but... ugh! We used protection, okay? I'm not a reckless teenager." Not that Gigi had ever been reckless when it came to sex. James had been her first and only until Sebastian. And James hadn't wanted kids any more than Gigi did, so he'd gotten snipped pretty early on. But up until then, they'd been careful.

"Thank the goddess," Carly said dramatically. "Can you imagine having a kid now? You're in your forties, right?"

Gigi nodded. "I'm not down for a geriatric pregnancy."

"I hear more and more women are waiting until they're in their late thirties and early forties to start having kids," Joy said. "There's nothing wrong with that if all the equipment is still working."

"Bite your tongue," Gigi and Carly said at the same time. Then they both started laughing.

"I guess we're in the no kids club together," Carly said to Gigi.

Gigi held her closed fist out to the actress and started to relax when Carly met it with her own for a fist bump of solidarity.

Joy shook her head at them. "The pair of you are like two peas in a pod. I think you have a lot in common with each other."

"She's not wrong," Carly said with a kind smile. "Between our mutual love for herbs and resistance to motherhood, we're practically soulmates."

Gigi snorted. "I can't argue with that." She leaned forward. "Now, tell me the honest truth about the products I sent over. Do you like them?"

Carly shook her head, looking solemn.

Gigi's heart sank. She'd been feeling so good about her products while working very hard to produce them, and now she was being told they weren't good enough. She glanced around the restaurant, looking for some sort of easy escape. But she didn't see one that wouldn't cause a giant commotion and bring a bunch of unwanted attention to Carly. Since escaping was out, she was left with hoping that the floor would open up and swallow her whole.

"I don't like your skin care line, Gigi; I *adore* it. Oh. Em. Gee. I am going to be able to sell the hell out of this stuff to my Hollywood girlfriends. Just hook me up with some samples, and the orders will fly in. I guarantee it."

Gigi sat there, momentarily stunned. She knew she had talent at what she did. But it was entirely another thing to hear from a movie star just how much she loved her product. "I... Thank you. I'm so glad you love it."

"It's by far the best skin care system I have ever tried, and that's saying something," Carly said. "I think I've tried every elixir out there at one time or another. This stuff? It's just so hydrating and great for sensitive skin. I swear, even my wrinkles started to fade."

"You don't have wrinkles," Joy said, rolling her eyes. "But I'm glad you're giving Gigi an ego boost. She deserves it."

All of Gigi's self-consciousness disappeared, and she beamed at them. "You two are excellent for a girl's ego. How about I return the favor?"

"Oh? Is this the part where you gush about Carly and beg for an autograph?" Joy asked, winking at Gigi.

"No. But it is the part where I tell Carly that her cellulite cream is amazing and that I'd like to add it to my line to be sold at Skyler's shop." She turned to Carly. "Only if you're interested, of course. You might not want to make that kind of commitment."

Carly's eyes lit up. "You think it's good?"

"It's great!" Joy said. "But I already told you that. Remember that dress that showed off my thigh at that gala I went to with Troy last week?"

"Yeah?"

"I couldn't have worn it without your cream. I would've had to wear a bodysuit, or maybe a bag over my head, so they were focused on something other than my dimpled thigh," Joy said.

Gigi laughed at her. "You're being a little dramatic, don't you think?"

Joy shook her head. "No way. That stuff is going to be gold for the over-forty crowd." She glanced at Carly. "Gigi knows it too; otherwise, she wouldn't be asking you if she can include it in her line."

Carly nodded. "I'd love to participate, but I'll need a contract and a little time for Sebastian to go over it."

"Of course." Gigi texted Skyler to let him know Carly was in. They'd already talked about it, and he was all for the cellulite cream that Carly had created. He'd basically said the same thing Joy had and was excited to see what the three of them could do. Then she texted Sebastian, telling him to hurry home the next day because she'd just made some work for him. Smiling to herself about their exchange earlier on the dating app, she wondered if he'd mention it. When he only confirmed that he'd be back by mid-afternoon, she decided she wouldn't bring it up either. It would be fun to keep the pretense up that they were strangers and to act as if they were going on their first date. For her, it added a level of playfulness she'd been missing in her life, and it just felt good.

"What are you smiling like that for?" Joy asked.

"Like what?" Gigi took a sip of her water and nodded to a waiter as he walked by, indicating they were ready to order. He held one finger up to let her know he'd be right back.

"You look all dreamy, like your heart is melting or something equally as sappy as that," Joy said, eyeing her.

"I'm just thinking about my date tomorrow night. And before you ask, that's all I'm going to tell you. Got it?"

Joy held her hands up in a surrender motion. "Yes, ma'am. But we're gonna want details later. You know that, right?"

"I'm starting to get the picture," Gigi deadpanned. She was about to tell them her lips would always be sealed, but the waiter arrived just at that moment, providing the perfect distraction.

"What can I get you ladies?" he asked.

"Plenty of wine, one red, two white," Joy said and then went on to order an obscene amount of food that the three of them could never finish.

Gigi sat back, her heart swelling with love and gratitude. A year ago, she'd have never imagined herself in this situation. Sure, she'd have gone out to dinner, but never with a coven mate and a movie star.

Life certainly was strange, Gigi thought. But with this new chosen family by her side, Gigi couldn't wait to see what else was in store for her.

CHAPTER NINETEEN

*G*igi spent her morning running errands before she stopped in at the Liminal Space Day Spa. It had been a while since she'd pampered herself. After getting her hair cut and highlighted to hide the few gray hairs that had started to make an appearance, she opted for a ninety-minute massage. By the time she made it back home, she felt like a goddess and couldn't wait for her date with Sebastian.

How had she gotten so lucky? He not only knew her inside and out, he was also the romantic she'd always wanted but hadn't had in her ex. Her phone buzzed with a text from Sebastian, making her heart flutter in her chest.

Looking forward to tonight. I've missed you.

She texted back that she missed him, too, and couldn't wait to stroll with him under the moonlight.

He sent back a heart emoji.

Gigi didn't continue to text him, knowing he was on the road from San Francisco. He'd told her earlier in the day that they had a breakthrough on tracking down who originally sold the ring to the auction house. He knew it had been done

DEANNA CHASE

through an LLC, but they still needed to track down who owned the company. He'd said that shouldn't take too long since most of those records were online. There was a good chance that by the time he arrived later in the evening that one of his researchers would've already found that information.

Time clicked by at a glacial speed. Gigi couldn't remember the last time she'd been so impatient for anything. Finally, at 11:45 p.m., she took one last look at herself in the mirror. Her flowy white dress was perfect. Her eyes were bright with excitement, and she couldn't stop the smile that was claiming her red lips. After pulling on a thick sweater, Gigi grabbed her house key, slipped out of her beach house, and took the trail down to the beach.

The almost-full moon reflected a shimmering silver sheen on the water, leaving her awed by the gorgeousness of the moment. With the sand beneath her feet and a slight breeze in her hair, Gigi decided she'd never been happier despite the chill in the air.

The walk from her home to Crescent beach wasn't far, and when she rounded the dunes, she immediately spotted Sebastian's SUV in the small parking area. He was early. She smiled to herself and kept walking, scanning the deserted beach for him.

There was nothing but moonlight, sand, and the sound of crashing waves. It wasn't often that Gigi was out at night on the beach, but she had to admit there was a peacefulness about it that called to her. Maybe she could talk Sebastian into celebrating the full moons out there on the beach. It could be their thing.

Once she passed a large rock outcropping, she spotted Sebastian. He was standing facing away from her, looking north. He was wearing a long black jacket and had a knit cap on his head. There was a blanket with a picnic basket right in the middle.

He looked so stoic, standing there with the beach backdrop and the moon highlighting him. She was silent as she walked up behind him and wrapped her arms around his waist. But as soon as she felt his body, alarm bells went off and she instantly sprang back and stumbled over the picnic basket, landing flat on her backside.

Frozen in place, she watched with wide eyes as the figure turned to look at her.

Her throat tightened, and the world narrowed to just the man standing over her with a self-satisfied smile on his face. Gigi had thought him attractive in his youth with his dark blond hair, green eyes, and angular jawbone. But now, all she saw was an abuser. He couldn't have been more unattractive if he tried.

"James," she finally forced out. "What are you doing here?"

"Isn't it obvious? I came to get my wife back." He kneeled down and held his hand out to her.

Gigi's flight instinct kicked in, and she scrambled back and onto her feet. The shock of seeing him had rendered her speechless at first, but now she had plenty to say. "Are you insane? We're divorced. You tried to beat the shit out of me. Do you really think I'd give you the time of day after everything that happened?"

"Now, Gigi. Don't be so dramatic." James took a step forward but stopped as soon as she stepped back. He let out a sigh. "Can't we just talk for a minute? Maybe take a walk and catch up?"

"I'm not going anywhere with you. How dare you? And where's Sebastian?" she demanded.

James stared her down, his expression full of pity. "You really are slow, aren't you?"

Rage surged through Gigi and she wanted nothing more than to deck the man standing in front of her, but if she attacked him, she'd never find out where Sebastian was or why James was there. "Clearly I've missed something. Why don't you fill me in?"

"Who do you think introduced you to that hard cider you demanded I keep stocked in the fridge? Or those apple turnovers that came from Aunt Helen's farm? You stopped eating those and drinking that cider after you gained twenty pounds and couldn't drop it. Did you really think your *boyfriend* had any idea about those two things?"

Gods, she hated him in that moment. He was right, of course. They had been together when she'd started on that kick. She just hadn't remembered exactly when it was or if Sebastian had still been in town. That meant that he'd somehow found out that she was on Exclusive and then catfished her. But how had he known? Surely he hadn't just been browsing and stumbled upon her profile. But that would mean he'd gotten to someone within her inner circle. Nausea made her mouth water, and she willed herself to not vomit. "Why?"

"Why what?" he asked, eyeing her thoughtfully.

"Why did you set up this elaborate scheme? Why pretend to be Sebastian while you messaged me on a dating app? Why did you lure me here to the beach at midnight?" She was shaking with anger as she added, "What is it you want from me?"

"You blocked my number, Gigi. Remember that? I had no way to contact you. If I'd messaged you as myself, would you have shown up tonight?"

"You could have knocked on my door," she said, just out of

spite. They both knew he'd never do that. Not as long as she lived in a haunted house where the ghosts had helped her kick his ass.

His nostrils flared with indignation as he asked, "Would you have answered?"

"No. But that's not an excuse to lure me here under false pretenses." She knew he was trying to hold back his temper. She wondered just how long he'd be able to keep himself under control and then decided she didn't want to find out. She glared at him and then turned on her heel and started to make her way back up the beach.

She felt rather than heard James chase after her. His hand wrapped around her arm, making her spin to face him.

"You are not running away from me again. I came here to talk, and that's what we're going to do," he said in a low, controlled voice.

"I have nothing to say to you, James. It's over. Go home." She yanked her arm out of his grip and tried not to look relieved when he actually let her go. He'd attacked her once before; there was no reason to believe that he wouldn't do it again.

He stuffed his hands in the pockets of his coat and hung his head, looking defeated.

Don't fall for this, Gigi, she told herself.

"I miss you. I miss *us*." He raised his head and looked at her imploringly. "Please, Gigi. Can't we just take a walk and talk for a few minutes? I want to apologize... for what happened."

There was no denying that Gigi desperately wanted an apology from this man. And not just for what happened that last day when he'd laid hands on her. They had over twenty years of toxic history that she'd spent the last nine months trying to reconcile. But would hearing those words from him change anything? She doubted it, but maybe she could try.

"Fine. You can walk me back toward my house. That's it," she said.

He nodded once and reached out, placing his hand on her hip as if he was going to guide her along.

Gigi immediately stepped away and said, "I'm not yours to touch anymore, James. Remember that."

"That's rich, considering you're sleeping with the man who has the answers to your mother's disappearance," he barked out, his face pinched in disgust.

Gigi just stared at her ex-husband with revulsion. "I can't believe you just said that. You know Sebastian had nothing to do with my mom's disappearance."

He raised a skeptical eyebrow. "Are you sure about that?"

A teeny-tiny voice in her head said, *no*. She shook her head, dislodging the traitorous thought. In her heart, she knew Sebastian was innocent. She would not let her creep of an ex-husband plant that doubt. "Go home, James. Wherever that is. I don't want you in my life."

"Fuck," he muttered and fell into step beside her.

Gigi pretended he wasn't there and hoped by the time they got to her house that he'd be too chickenshit to get close.

"I messed up," he said. "I know that. But don't we owe it to ourselves to at least talk about what happened? Try to forgive each other?"

No matter how much she wanted to ignore him, there was no way she could let that comment go. "Forgive each other? What exactly did I do that needs forgiveness? I'm not the one who attacked you."

"I already told you I regret that. I've gone to therapy over it, you know."

She didn't know that, but it changed nothing. If he had actually gotten help, then good for him. But she was under no obligation to forgive him.

"I learned a lot there," he said. "I know now that I was selfish and didn't pay enough attention to us. I'm a large part of the reason we grew apart. But I also learned that you weren't exactly emotionally available to me, and that's why I had those affairs. If we could—"

"Stop right there, you arrogant asshole. I'm not to blame for you sticking your dick in other women," she spat out. "Don't ever say that something I did or didn't do was the reason you cheated on me. You're responsible for you, and I'm responsible for me. End of story. I never cheated on you. I never put you at risk for disease. I never once held you back from anything. So get back in the SUV you spent far too much to rent just so you could impersonate my boyfriend, and leave me alone. I owe you nothing." She took off down the beach, tired of listening to his bullshit. As it turned out, she didn't even want an apology from him. All she wanted was for him to disappear.

"Gigi!" he called.

She sped up, cursing herself because ever since her yoga disaster she hadn't been brave enough to try working out again. Running on the beach was likely to kill her. She was breathing heavily, and her legs were starting to burn when someone—James—tackled her from behind. She went down with an *oomph*, face-first into the sand. "Get off me!" she ordered, kicking and rolling to try to shake him off.

"No, Gigi," he said into her ear. "You're mine, and you owe me. Now relax, or else I'm going to have to get rough with you."

"Get rough? You just tackled me, you prick." She jerked her head back, knocking her skull right into his nose.

"Ouch! You bitch!" He rolled off her, and she quickly got to her feet, trying to scramble to get away, but he grabbed her hair and yanked, causing her to fall to her knees. "I think you broke my nose."

"Good," she said through clenched teeth. "Now let me go before I call my spirits."

"Don't act like I'm an idiot. I know they're confined to the house." He yanked harder, making her wince in pain.

If he thought his tactics were going to make her cooperate, he was stupider than she'd thought. She wanted to reach out and punch him in the balls, but she wasn't in a good position. Besides, if he was working this hard to not let her go, he wanted something. She'd be better served if she figured out what that might be.

Gigi went completely still and looked up at him, searching his expression in the darkness. He was obviously angry, but there was something else beneath the surface—desperation. "Oh, gods," she said. "You've come here because you want more money."

James's eyes widened and then narrowed. "What makes you say that?"

"I know you," she sneered. "How much to make you go away?"

He stared down at her with a carefully blank face. "One million. Then you'll never see me again."

Holy mother of all that was precious. Was he for real? She'd already paid him off for a quick divorce mere months ago. Yet here he was demanding money again. If she said yes and actually gave him the cash, there was nothing to stop him from coming after her again. But if she said yes now, he'd at least let her go long enough to get the cashier's check. "Fine. You'll sign a contract indicating that you won't sue in the future for more alimony, and I'll get you the check."

"I already signed one of those. No need."

She knew differently. As soon as she opened her wallet, she knew that would open her up to more litigation. "It's the only way you're getting that check."

"Fine. It's a deal." He tightened his grip on her hair, making her wince. "But so help me, Gigi, if you're fucking with me, I promise I will make your life miserable. Got it?"

She tried to nod, but his grip on her hair was too tight.

"Say you understand," he ordered.

"I understand," she echoed.

He let go, and she slumped into the sand, holding her head with both hands as she massaged her scalp with her fingers. When she stood, she stared him straight in the eye and said, "Don't ever touch me again, James. Do you understand?"

He scoffed. "I didn't hurt you."

Gigi was done being shocked by his ugliness. But she was shocked by her own unadulterated rage. It swelled up from the depths of her soul and without any brain input from her, she curled her hand into a fist, felt magic flood her arm, and then landed a very impressive right hook that knocked him out cold.

CHAPTER TWENTY

*G*igi was shaking with left over adrenaline as she hurried toward her house, holding her aching fist against her body. All she wanted to do was get inside where she knew she'd have the protection of her spirits.

"Gigi?" Sebastian's strained voice rang through the night.

"Sebastian?" she forced out around a sob. "You're here?"

Suddenly he appeared out from behind the arbor that framed the walkway to her house. His arms circled around her and he pulled her in close. "What happened? What's wrong?"

Gigi clung to him and shook her head. She wasn't going to be able to get the story out. Not yet. Through halting breaths, she said, "Inside. I need... inside."

There was no hesitation. He lifted her in his arms and strode up the front walk and then set her on her feet. Her hands were shaking as she tried to unlock the front door, and when she dropped the key, Sebastian retrieved it and let them inside.

The minute her feet hit the wood floors she felt the presence of the Hannigan sisters. The warmth of their concern wrapped around her like an invisible blanket, calming her. She'd stopped shaking, but the surreal experience of fighting her ex on the beach kept running like a loop in her mind.

"Gigi?" Sebastian placed a gentle hand on her cheek. "What happened, baby?"

She lifted her gaze to his and couldn't stop the tears from spilling down her cheeks as she said, "James is back."

Wind gushed through her house, slamming doors and knocking over a vase that shattered on her floor. Pictures flew from the walls while Gigi stood with Sebastian in the middle of it all, safe in a small bubble where nothing touched them.

When the Hannigan sisters showed no sign of slowing down, Gigi took a small step away from Sebastian and said, "Thank you. Your outrage has not gone unnoticed. I doubt he'd come here because he's afraid of you, but if he does, he's all yours."

The violent wind stopped, and a soft chuckled rippled through the air and faded away along with the presence of the Hannigan sisters. The loss of their energy made Gigi's knees buckle, and if it hadn't been for Sebastian's strong arms grabbing her, she'd have ended up sprawled on the floor.

"Damn, Gigi. Those are some fierce spirits you have watching over you," Sebastian whispered in her ear as he wrapped his arms around her again.

She nodded, knowing they were better than any security system she could buy on the market. Their presence even at the mention of James's name was a real eye-opener for her. She'd been wondering what, if anything, they thought of Sebastian. Since they'd not only protected her, but they'd protected him too from their wrath that evening, she knew they approved. If they didn't, she doubted he'd be welcome in the house.

They stood there just holding each other for a bit until Sebastian pulled back and asked, "Are you going to tell me what happened?"

"I knocked James out cold and left him lying face-first in the sand," she blurted.

Sebastian blinked at her. "You did what?"

"He... He hurt me, so I clocked him," she said, staring at her feet.

"Where?" he growled.

"Crescent Beach." She waved a hand toward the sea below her house. "Right by the small parking lot there."

Sebastian turned on his heel and headed for the door. On his way out, he called over his shoulder, "I'll be back as soon as I can."

Gigi was still in her living room as she watched him leave. When the door slammed closed behind him, she pointed herself toward her stairs and then made a beeline for her shower.

The hot water sluiced over her aching muscles and eased the tension in her shoulders. Her scalp was tender, and her back ached from the altercation. Her legs weren't feeling much better after her attempt to run on the beach.

The echo of his demand kept replaying over and over in her mind. There was plenty of money in the trust, but if she decided to give it to him, what would that mean in the future? And if she didn't, what would that mean for her present? Would James keep popping up in random places to squeeze her out of more cash? She had no reason to believe he wouldn't. He was that kind of douche.

Gigi didn't know how long she'd been in the shower, but she was still there when Sebastian returned a short time later. Without a word, he stripped out of his clothes and joined her.

He stood behind her, his arm wrapped around her and his larger body framing hers.

Being held by him in the safety of her house made her feel safe for the first time that evening.

"Tell me you didn't kill him," Gigi said, closing her eyes and leaning her head against his chest.

Sebastian had one arm wrapped around her stomach and the other around her chest. "Nope. Unfortunately."

Gigi knew she should feel relieved that he hadn't done anything that would put him on the wrong side of the law. But she didn't. All she felt was despair. "What did you say to him?"

"Nothing. He wasn't there." Sebastian nuzzled his face into her neck. "No car. No man. No traces."

"Dammit," Gigi said, feeling like a failure. "I should have called the police." Not that they would have gotten to the beach any sooner. She'd had no way to call them until she got home since she hadn't taken her phone with her. That's what she'd intended to do, but the moment she saw Sebastian, all her good intentions flew out the window.

"It wouldn't have made a difference," he said, echoing her thoughts. He reached over and turned the water off. "Let's get you out of here before your entire body turns into a prune."

Gigi looked down at her fingers and winced when she saw the wrinkled digits. No doubt she had other parts that hadn't faired any better. She let him lead her out of the shower, dry her off, and tuck her into bed.

Once Sebastian was beside her, he spooned her from the back and whispered, "What happened tonight?"

Gigi took a deep breath, and while wrapped in his arms, she told him everything.

* * *

THE SOUND of pounding on the front door along with the incessant ringing of the doorbell woke Gigi from a deep sleep. She sat bolt upright, rubbing at her grainy eyes. It had been really late when she and Sebastian had finally gone to sleep. They'd talked long into the night about what to do about James, but they hadn't come up with much of a solid plan. They would file a police report just to get the incident on record, but Gigi and Sebastian knew nothing would come of it. Since Gigi wasn't hurt worse physically, they'd take the complaint, but there were no guarantees that any of it would make it into his file. There wasn't really anything to do other than wait to see what he did next.

And Sebastian hated that. He'd wanted to track him down and threaten him within an inch of his life. Gigi secretly enjoyed that conversation. She'd give anything to see Sebastian tear James apart, but she didn't want him to lose his ability to practice law because he was jealous or pissed off over James's bullshit.

The doorbell rang again, followed by what sounded like elephants at the front door. When she finally got the door open, Skyler rushed in with Autumn right behind him.

"Oh my god! Gigi, are you okay?" He scanned her body, looking for bruises or other wounds. "I can't believe that bastard showed up here."

Gigi shut the door and turned around to greet her morning visitors. "How do you know about last night?"

"Pete and I have security cameras," Skyler said with a wave of his hand, dismissing her concern. He gently picked up her right hand and kissed the bruised knuckles. "I'm so proud of you, baby girl. From what we could see, you really gave him hell."

Gigi's lips twitched in slight amusement. The topic wasn't

funny, but her friends were sweet and adorable. "Come in. I need coffee ASAP."

Skyler glanced around her living room and let out a gasp of horror. He grabbed Gigi's good hand, delaying her from getting to the coffee maker. "What happened in here? It looks like that last scene in *Ghostbusters* right before they save the day."

"The Hannigan sisters weren't too happy when they learned James returned," Gigi said. "But don't worry, they didn't hurt anyone. It was just me and Sebastian here when that went down."

Skyler hurried after her as Gigi finally found her way into the kitchen. She was on autopilot as she made the coffee and then sat on a stool next to Skyler as they waited. It was then she realized that Autumn was still there. She'd noticed her when she'd opened the door, but what she didn't know was why she was there at all. Gigi leaned over and asked Skyler why the woman was in her kitchen at eight-thirty in the morning.

"We were working at the house," Skyler said indignantly. "That is where my design studio is after all."

"Right, of course." She turned to Autumn. "Are you helping with the designing end, too?"

"Maybe," Skyler answered for her. "We're still working that out. Today we were sorting through higher-end used clothes I picked up while you were down in Fairytown or wherever it was you grew up. Pete told me there was an alert on our security system, so that's when I took a look and saw you clock that douchebucket. Nice right hook!"

"Thanks," she said sheepishly and flexed her fingers. But then it dawned on her that Skyler actually had the whole thing recorded. "Did you see what happened to him after I left?"

"You rang his bell pretty hard. When he got up, he stumbled to his SUV, which I thought was Sebastian's at first until I saw the rental tag. Anyway, he stumbled over, made a phone call, and then drove off."

"He made a phone call?" Sebastian asked from the kitchen doorway. He was leaning against the doorjamb, shirtless.

Skyler's eyes nearly bugged out as he stared, while Autumn looked away.

Gigi couldn't help but chuckle. "Put a shirt on. You're distracting the neighbor."

Sebastian rolled his eyes, disappeared for a few minutes and then returned with a T-shirt on. "Better?" he asked Gigi.

"No," Skyler chimed in.

Gigi nodded and handed him the first cup of coffee.

"Thanks." He turned to Skyler. "We're gonna need those tapes. They will come in handy for the police report we'll file today."

"Of course," Skyler said, gratefully accepting his own cup of coffee.

Once Gigi and Autumn had a cup, the four of them went into the dining room where they sat around the table. They filled Skyler and Autumn in on Gigi's ordeal the night before and waited patiently while Skyler cursed under his breath and made vague references about poisonous herbs. Autumn was quiet and didn't say anything at all as she studied her cooling coffee.

"Autumn? Is everything okay?" Gigi asked her.

The other woman raised her weary eyes to Gigi's and said, "Yes. It's just so awful. I don't know why it is that men like that always seem to get away with so much awful crap."

Gigi rubbed her shoulder, understanding that Autumn had

her own experience with an abusive partner or authority figure.

"He's not going to get away with it. Not this time," Sebastian promised.

They dropped the subject of James, much to everyone's relief, and after a moment, Gigi turned to Sebastian and said, "I forgot to ask about what you found out in San Francisco. You said you had a lead."

"Right." Sebastian ran a hand through his hair and leaned back in his chair as he said, "We got the name of the LLC that sold your ring to the auction house. It's called Mystical Finds of Avalon if you can believe that."

Autumn let out a gasp and quickly covered her mouth with both hands.

"Autumn?" Gigi asked, concerned. "What is it?"

"Do you know that company?" Sebastian added.

Autumn gave a slow nod. When she finally spoke, she said, "It belongs to my father."

CHAPTER TWENTY-ONE

"Your father!" Gigi jumped out of her chair, needing to put space between her and Autumn. How was this real? What exactly was Autumn doing there? Was she a plant by her father for some reason? Is that why she showed up right at the same time that Gigi had started to look for answers about her mother's disappearance again? She narrowed her eyes at the other woman. "Why are you here?"

"Gigi," Skyler said, a gentle warning in his tone. "Don't you think we should give her a second to explain?"

"Don't you think it's just a little too much of a coincidence?" Gigi demanded. There was a small voice inside her head that was warning her that she was overreacting, that there was some other reason this was happening, but she ignored it. She was too upset to follow her intuition. "I mean, how did she just end up in Premonition Pointe and working for my best friend? Hell, she's even here the morning after James catfished me."

"It does look bad," Autumn said, her face white. "I don't

know how to explain any of this, but you should know I haven't spoken to my father in many years."

Convenient, Gigi thought. After her experience the night before, her ability to take anyone at their word was nonexistent. "I'm sorry. I just don't know that I can trust you."

You can, a voice whispered seemingly from nowhere. *Listen to her.*

Gigi glanced around, and when she saw nothing, she yelled in frustration, "If you know something, just tell me. Stop with the cryptic messages and unexplained advice!"

Autumn, who'd been shrinking away from Gigi, suddenly got to her feet and stared Gigi in the eye. "I'm not like my father. I've done everything in my power to get away from him ever since I was a teenager, so I have no idea why his company is involved in selling a ring your mother was wearing the day she disappeared. How could I? Is it strange that this is happening? Yes. But that's not my fault, and the only reason I'm here is because I'm working with Skyler. Or at least I was." She turned to him. "Unless you've changed your mind."

Skyler glanced at Gigi. She gave him a noncommittal shrug. That wasn't her decision to make, though she'd be uncomfortable with Autumn until she knew more about her father and how he obtained her mother's ring. Skyler turned back to Autumn and said, "You know Gigi is my best friend, right?"

"Fine. I'll go," Autumn said.

"Wait!" Skyler ran around in front of her, blocking her path to the door. "I didn't say I've changed my mind. You're a great assistant, and so far, I've seen no reason to believe that you're... I don't know, trying to infiltrate our group or something. I'm the one who came to find you, right? I begged you to come work for me after seeing the work you'd done on the Thorne estate sale. Let's just talk this out and figure out where we go from here."

Autumn pressed her lips together in a thin line. Her jaw was clenched, and there was no mistaking the frustrated anger written all over her. "I'm sorry, Skyler, I just don't think this is a good idea." She darted around Skyler and made a beeline for the door. Once she was in the threshold, she glanced over her shoulder, and in an icy tone she said, "You know, I did everything in my power to distance myself from my bigoted father. It's gut-wrenching to once again be forced to walk away from something because he's a total piece of shit. But I won't sit around and wait to be accepted. I've done that far too many times in my life, and I'm done with that now. Good luck, Gigi. I hope you find what you're looking for."

The door slammed behind her, and everyone turned to stare at Gigi.

"Dammit." Gigi ran after her, knowing she'd messed up. Sure, she'd been shocked to hear the connection, but Autumn had been the one to offer the information. Why would she do that if she was some kind of spy? Then there was the fact that she'd just looked so broken while talking about her father. Gigi knew all too well what it was like to have a shit father. She'd been abandoned by her own before she was even old enough to remember him.

"Autumn!" Gigi called from her driveway. The other woman was already next door at Skyler's and climbing into a small red hatchback car. "Please don't go!"

Autumn glanced over at her for a second, but then shook her head and disappeared into her car.

"Way to go, Gigi. Looks like you're in the running for the asshole of the year award," Gigi muttered to herself as she took off running, trying to reach Autumn before she sped off down the road.

Autumn had just started to back out of Skyler's driveway when Gigi ran over, waving her arms. "Please. Just give me a chance to apologize and explain." There was no way Autumn heard her latest plea. The window was rolled up, and the wind was blowing harder than normal. But the car came to a stop anyway.

When Autumn didn't kill the engine or get out of the car, Gigi pushed her hair out of her eyes, walked up to the window, and mouthed, *Please?*

Gigi saw Autumn visibly sigh just before she threw her hands up and then put the car in park. A moment later, she got out of the car, her face pinched and her shoulders tensed.

"All right," Autumn said. "You have two minutes before I get back in my car and go. I promised myself a long time ago that I was never going to force myself on people who won't accept me or see me for who I am."

"I'm sorry," Gigi said at once. "I'm not in a great place mentally this morning, and trying to navigate my past and anyone potentially connected to it is kind of messy. I'd like it if you'd come back inside and talk with us."

"Why?" Autumn crossed her arms over her chest, looking defiant. "So you can grill me about my father? I'll warn you now that I haven't spoken to him in over ten years and don't know much about his business. He wasn't exactly the kind to think a daughter might take over his empire one day. It was his greatest disappointment that he didn't have a son."

Gigi closed her eyes and sucked in a breath. When she opened them, she met Autumn's gaze and said, "I really am sorry. I'd like you to come back in because you're Skyler's assistant. He'll kill me if I let you leave like this. But also, and more importantly, I want you to come back because I *do* like you and I wasn't being fair. Yes, I'm sure anything you can share about your father would be helpful, but it isn't necessary if you don't want to talk about him. Sebastian has private investigators he can call who will get the information we need."

Autumn dropped her arms to her sides and then held her hands palms up. "All right. But mostly for Skyler. He's been very kind to me. I don't want to upset him."

Gigi smiled at her. "He really is the best, isn't he?"

Autumn nodded and fell into step beside Gigi as they went back to Gigi's house.

Skyler was waiting for them on the front porch, and when they got close, he placed his hands on his hips and stared Gigi down. "It's a damned good thing you got her to come back, because if she'd quit, I'd have had to put a giant flamingo in your yard just to piss you off."

Gigi chuckled. He knew how much she despised the plastic pink flamingos. James had always wanted them in the yard, but about the fourth time she'd been approached about swinging with Hollywood insiders, she'd lost her shit and trashed them all. James, the obstinate jackass that he was, purchased twice as many the next day and arranged them in compromising positions. Looking back, it was almost funny. But at the time, she'd been mortified. He hadn't taken them down for months just to torture her.

"Pink flamingos?" Autumn asked.

"It's a long story," Gigi said. "But trust me, I'd have been horrified. So now you know how to get under my skin." She jerked her head toward the door. "Let's go in and get more coffee. I don't know about you guys, but for me it's definitely going to be a two-cup day."

"Two-cup?" Skyler scoffed. "More like a two-pot day."

Gigi slipped her arm through his and said, "I bet Sebastian has something already brewed."

Sure enough, Sebastian not only had another pot of coffee ready, but he'd also laid out a platter of bagels and a few different kinds of cream cheese. Gigi gave him a grateful smile and took her place at the table.

Sebastian sat beside her and reached over, taking her hand. "You sure you're okay?"

Gigi nodded. "I will be." Eventually. Maybe. She leaned against him, just grateful he was there.

Skyler and Autumn chatted for a few minutes. When they returned to the table, Skyler had his arm around her shoulders. He gave her a quick kiss on the cheek and said, "Of course you can bring a date to the opening. Why would that even be a question?"

"I just wasn't sure if I'd be working or mingling," she said. "I didn't want Zoe to be on her own all night."

Her, Gigi thought. Hadn't Autumn mentioned having a stalkerish ex-boyfriend before? Though that didn't mean anything. She had known plenty of bi people in Hollywood.

"She won't be on her own. Your job will actually be to mingle, so if you can do that together, it's great," Skyler said. "Pete will be there, too. If something goes terribly wrong and we're busy, they can hang together."

"Okay. Thanks." Autumn sat at the table and fired off a text, smiling for the first time since Gigi had accused her of being a spy.

"Skyler?" Sebastian said.

"Yeah?"

"Do you think I could see the security footage from last night before we hand it over to the cops?"

"Sure." Skyler pulled his phone out and started tapping on the screen.

Gigi frowned. "Why do you want to see that?"

He raised his eyebrows, looking surprised. "Why wouldn't I? I want to see what the video captured so I know what kind of evidence they'll have. If it's weak, they might have a hard time building a case. I'd rather know that upfront."

"Right," she said, knowing that his attorney side had kicked in. It made sense that he wanted to see it. But Gigi didn't. Not one bit. "I'm going to sit this one out. But you two go ahead."

Skyler propped his phone against a mug and hit play. There wasn't much sound other than wind and a couple of faint cries. Still, it made Gigi wince as she had to relive the attack. Gigi got up and started to pace. Unable to keep her cool, she started to fidget, and her breathing sped up.

Autumn jumped up from her chair and hurried over to Gigi. She spoke in a low voice when she said, "You're okay. You're safe now. Your ex can't touch you." She turned and waved toward the video. "It's just a—holy shit. I thought you said your ex's name was James."

"It is," Gigi said. "Why?"

Autumn walked up behind Sebastian and took a long look at the video. After a moment, she let out a gasp and said, "It's him. That's PJ."

"PJ?" They all said at once.

"My—" She stopped and stared at Gigi, her expression horrified.

"Your what?" Gigi asked, feeling her stomach drop to the floor. Whatever she was going to say, Gigi knew it was going to be way worse than finding out her father's company was involved in the sale of her mother's ring.

She shook her head, her mouth working, but no sound coming out.

"Brother? Boyfriend? UPS driver?" Gigi filled in, trying to keep it together.

"Boyfriend," she finally forced out. "The one who became a stalker."

CHAPTER TWENTY-TWO

"*Y*our stalker?" Gigi gasped out. "How? When?"

Autumn stared at Skyler's phone, shock quickly morphing to pure rage as her lips turned into a scowl and her fingers into fists. "I dated him for a few months, and then when I realized we weren't going to be compatible, I cut him off. After that he started following me, leaving me creepy gifts at work, and showing up at my apartment, acting as if we had plans when we didn't. I swear it was an elaborate effort to gaslight me."

Gigi shared a glance with Sebastian. When she saw Sebastian's skeptical look, she said, "He told her his name is PJ. James's given name is Preston James."

"Fuck!" Sebastian ran a frustrated hand through his hair. "This doesn't make any sense."

"Tell me about it," Autumn spat out. "How is it that I'm suddenly in the middle of all of this drama?"

"Autumn, when did this happen?" Gigi asked. She was well past suspecting Autumn of any nefarious activity. If her current reaction was an act, then the woman deserved an Oscar. She was one thousand percent freaked out.

Autumn drew in a shaky breath. "It ended three months ago. It started right after I got to town. I met him on a dating app." She let out a snort. "He didn't even use a current photo. They were all from at least fifteen years ago. I should've ditched him then, but he was really charming. The kind of person who just oozes charisma. For the first month, I just thought he was amazing. But then he started talking about getting serious and wanting to move in together and share bank accounts. I just really wasn't into that, so I told him it was too fast. When he wouldn't let it go, I ended it. I have issues with being pressured."

"I wish I had been as smart as you when he did the same thing to me twenty some years ago," Gigi said, relating to everything Autumn just said. James *was* charming and knew how to get what he wanted. But when it didn't work on Gigi anymore, he'd moved on to someone else. The only thing that confused her was that Gigi didn't see him dating someone without a large bank account. "Autumn, did he know who your father is?"

"Yeah. He asked me about my family, and since he was easy to talk to, I told him about my nonexistent relationship with my father. Why?"

"Just a hunch. He was probably after your money, because that's who he is." Gigi was willing to bet her bank account balance that he'd known who she was before he took her out and thought if he could get together with the daughter, then he'd have access to a fortune again.

"The joke's on him," she said, shaking her head. "My father cut me off years ago. I was supposed to have a trust fund that kicked in this year, but he changed that, too." She shrugged. "Doesn't matter. I don't want anything from him anyway."

Gigi contemplated that for a bit. It was likely James didn't have any of that information and just went after someone he assumed had access to money. It was all he really cared about. "We need to go make a report. This can't wait. We need to tell the police all of it. What happened last night and what happened to Autumn."

Autumn nodded. "He's clearly dangerous. I did try to file a complaint a couple months ago when he wouldn't leave me alone, but they didn't take me seriously. They said there was nothing they could do unless he physically harmed me. Bullshit, right?"

Most definitely. Gigi wanted to scream. Why was it that creepers could get away with mentally torturing someone and it was only a problem after they physically harmed the person they were stalking? "It's a fucked-up situation for sure."

"We at least need to get it on the record," Sebastian said. "It will help strengthen the case once it does escalate. Come on. We'll all go together."

"WELL, that was a complete waste of time," Gigi said, flinging herself into a chair at the Bird's Eye Bakery. They'd spent three hours at the police station giving statements and filing a report. The deputy who spoke with them was kind enough but didn't seem to think the two incidents were related in any way other than it being the same person. He seemed to think that since James had eventually left Autumn alone, he'd go away and stop harassing Gigi as well. When Gigi said she wanted to press charges for the assault, he said he'd hand it over to the DA but didn't seem convinced the DA would do much with it.

"No, it wasn't a waste of time. We have the report on record. It could come in handy later," Sebastian said, sitting next to her and covering her hand with his.

"When it's too late," Autumn muttered.

"I agree," Skyler added. "We can't just wait to see what he does next. We have to do something."

"I can put a tail on him," Sebastian said. "Watch his movements. See what he's up to. Gigi, do you know where he's working these days?"

"If he hasn't changed jobs, then yes." She grabbed her phone and sent the information to him in an email. "That should get you started. He moved at the same time I did, but I don't know his address. I could probably get it from my divorce attorney."

Autumn cleared her throat. "He was staying in a short-term rental when we were dating while he looked for a place. I don't know if he's still there though. I can text you the address."

"Perfect. That's a start." Sebastian grabbed his phone and got to his feet. "I'm going to make a call and get someone started on that. I'll be right back."

With Sebastian gone, they all fell silent. Gigi had an overwhelming feeling of doom. Something told her it wasn't a coincidence that he'd targeted Autumn. There was a connection somewhere, but she wasn't seeing it. "Autumn, what did James tell you about himself?"

She frowned. "Let's see. That he was in advertising. He did a lot of name-dropping and seemed surprised when I was unimpressed. My dad had a lot of high-powered friends. They were all assholes, so that's not a life I care to ever be associated with."

Gigi let out a snort. "Yes, he is obsessed with money and power."

"He also told me that his, quote, 'bitch of an ex-wife' tried to take him to the cleaners, but that he managed to escape without losing too much of his fortune, thank the gods." She grimaced. "Real charmer. It was around then that I decided he wasn't the one for me."

"That's rich," Gigi said, shaking her head. Then she let out a humorous bark of laughter. How in the world had she ever been snowed by him? "He didn't have anything when we got married. The money he has now is from our divorce settlement, courtesy of my family's trust."

"I think he might be running out," Autumn said. "There were signs that he might be overextended."

"You're kidding." Gigi's eyes widened. It would take real stupidity to run through that much money in just a few short months.

"I don't know for sure, but I think his car was repossessed. And I saw a couple of late notices in his mail. He said he had a banking issue and he'd already taken care of it. There were just too many things that raised red flags."

"He sounds desperate," Skyler said. "But why? What did he do with Gigi's settlement? Autumn, we already know he just stopped harassing you one day. Do you know why?"

She shook her head. "No. I thought maybe it was because I complained to the police. If they questioned him at all or if he'd been tailing me and saw me go in, maybe that scared him off? Or maybe he realized he was targeting me for money that was never going to materialize."

"Maybe," Gigi said. "He's kind of a coward. He wouldn't like it if the police started questioning him. It would look bad to his clients."

Skyler nodded. "It's possible today's trip to the police station will get him to leave Gigi alone, but they have a much longer history. And if he needs money, that could turn into a dangerous situation. If he has a desperate need for cash, then he doesn't have time to finesse himself into another relationship with someone who has tons of money to burn. That leaves Gigi as his best option. He knows her and knows if he can wear her down, he'll get what he needs."

"That sounds like a decent theory," Sebastian said, slipping back into his seat. "I've got one of my best guys working on him. And another working to find out how Mystical Finds of Avalon obtained Carolyn's ring. I'm not sure there's anything else to do until we hear back from one or both of them."

Gigi sat back in her chair, feeling like they'd done everything they could for the moment but also like they were missing something vital. But no matter how hard she tried to run through it all in her head, she came up blank. There was nothing to do now but wait.

CHAPTER TWENTY-THREE

"*A*nything?" Gigi asked Sebastian as they strolled Main Street. They'd just met up for dinner after Gigi spent the day stocking Skyler's boutique with her skin care line. The soft opening was just three days away, and she wanted to make sure she'd made enough product to not only fill the shelves, but to have extra on hand to restock. It turned out she had a decent amount, but she wanted to make more just to be on the safe side.

Sebastian blew out a frustrated breath. "I can't get ahold of Gage, the PI who's researching Mystical Finds of Avalon. Last I heard from him, he did confirm that Emerson Sanders is the owner. But it appears that particular business was shuttered over five years ago. Gage was going to dig deeper and call me this morning. There's been radio silence, and honestly, I'm getting really concerned about him. He never goes off grid without warning."

"Did you hear from John?" Gigi's stomach had been in knots ever since the morning after James had attacked her. She hadn't heard anything from him, which might mean he actually was laying low because they went to the police, but that intuition of hers just would not shut up. Something was very wrong. She just didn't know what.

"Yes. He said James is having money issues. His credit is in the toilet. He doesn't know why, but he's still trying to work it out. He also said that other than going to his job at the advertising firm, he hasn't left his house all week."

That was good. At least he wasn't out terrorizing anyone else. "I know that should reassure me, but it just doesn't. Something is up. I can feel it."

He took her hand and raised it and brushed his lips over her knuckles. "Intuition is a powerful tool. But it's hard to take action on a feeling."

He seemed just as frustrated as she felt.

Gigi let out a sigh. "I'm not going to be able to relax at a restaurant. What do you say we get takeout and head to the beach?"

"Sounds good." After getting sandwiches at the Earthly Spirits Deli, they headed down toward the water. There were a few people walking the shoreline, but since it was a weekday, they had most of the beach to themselves. Instantly, as Gigi stepped onto the sand, she felt some of the tension drain from her.

"The beach is where you recharge, isn't it?" Sebastian said.

She nodded. "It's that obvious?"

"Yes." He smiled down at her. "The tension just seems to drain from your entire body when you're down here. The transformation happens almost immediately."

"You never noticed when we were kids?" she asked. "This isn't new."

"No, but you carry more with you now, so I think that's why I can see it now but didn't then." He frowned. "Did we never go to the beach after your mom disappeared?"

She shook her head. "No. I couldn't. Not for a long time. It was too hard. The beach was where Mom and I really talked. We'd take walks in the evenings, and that's when we communicated. After she disappeared, I just couldn't. It hurt too much. It took me many years to get back to loving the beach."

Sebastian stopped in one of the coves that protected them from the breeze, wrapped his arms around her and gave her a soft, slow kiss. When he pulled away, he said, "I'm glad you found your way back. It seems like you're doing that a lot lately."

She knew he was talking about her finding her way back to him. "And how do you feel about that?"

"Is that a serious question?" he asked with one eyebrow raised.

"Yes."

"I feel like I got the love of my life back and I don't ever want to lose her again."

Dammit. Tears stung her eyes. "Are you trying to make me cry?"

He shook his head. "No. I'm just trying to let you know I'm all in on this, Gigi. Whatever we find, however this turns out, I'm all in."

There was no stopping the single tear that rolled down her cheek. "I'm all in, too. This time, I'm not letting you go."

His lips curved into a slow smile, and then he dipped his head and kissed her with everything he had.

"Well, well, well," a familiar and very unwelcome voice said.

"Isn't this just the sweetest thing anyone has ever seen. Two star-crossed lovers, finally coming together to defeat the evil ex. What a clichéd storyline."

Gigi jerked away from Sebastian and spun, coming face to face with James. He was wearing that same black jacket he'd had on the night he'd attacked her, and in the light of day, she noticed that he was wearing clothes that looked exactly like Sebastian's. He had the same dark blue jeans and green button-down shirt. Even the brown loafers were an exact match. "What the hell are you doing here?"

"Gigi, no." Sebastian stepped in front of her just as James raised his arm and jabbed a needle into Sebastian's neck. Sebastian instantly fell to the sand in a heap of limbs.

"What the hell did you just do?" Gigi cried, dropping to her knees to check on Sebastian. He was unconscious, but to her relief he was still breathing. She held Sebastian and glared up at James, who'd shrugged out of his coat. "James! Answer me!" she demanded.

He didn't answer as he yanked her up by the arm and threw the coat over Sebastian's body.

"No!" Gigi slammed her foot down on James's instep and tried to elbow him in the gut, but he moved quickly, avoiding her attack, and twisted her arm until he had it restrained against her back.

"Try that again and I'll break your arm," he hissed into her ear.

"Why are you doing this?" she asked, staring at Sebastian's lifeless body.

"Because, Gigi, you're mine, and I will not stand by and let that piece of shit get his hooks into you. Now be a nice girl, or I'll jab this needle into you next."

Gigi felt the cold, sharp tip of the needle against her neck and decided right then and there that she would not let James take her without a fight, even if it meant he drugged her. She knew that he wasn't going to kill her. He wanted something, and if she died, he wasn't going to get it. "You're a coward," she whispered.

"If you say so. But I'm not the one whimpering over someone who's responsible for your mother's death." His voice was ice cold, but that wasn't what sent the chill up her spine. He'd just said her mother was dead. Never once in the time that they'd been together had they ever referred to her mother as anything but missing.

"What did you just say?" she snarled back.

"You heard me. If it wasn't for him, she'd still be alive. Now move and act like we're on a stroll. I don't want any more incriminating videos taken of us. If one more cop comes to my door, I'll make sure you're punished for it. Got it?"

He was holding her arm so tightly that she was sure if either of them moved another inch, he was going to snap it in two. Waiting for her moment to act, she nodded and said, "Yeah. Fine. I get it."

His grip tightened on her arm, making her wince. "Don't play me, Gigi. I know how you operate."

"I'm not," she gasped out. "Please, you're hurting me. I'll do what you ask."

"You better, or remember, I'll shoot you so full of this drug you won't wake up for a week." He released her, pushing her forward so that she fell to her knees. She immediately reached for Sebastian but was yanked back by her hair... again. The pain made tears sting her eyes. She blinked rapidly, trying to keep her vision clear. He positioned himself so that he was behind her. "Get up. Don't turn around or else I'll be carrying you out of here. Got it?"

"Yeah," she gasped.

He let go, and Gigi got to her feet, holding her arm against her middle. He'd yanked it so hard that she had no doubt it would be bruised.

"Now walk just in front of me."

Gigi started to go back the way she'd come, but he barked, "The other way. Down the beach away from prying eyes."

Swallowing hard, Gigi glanced one last time at Sebastian and then did as she was told.

"That's a good girl. Now—"

Gigi clasped both hands together and spun with her arms out, aiming for his head. Her hands connected just as she'd hoped, but he dodged to the side, avoiding most of the blow, and Gigi stumbled to the sand. "Shit!"

"I told you not to—"

She reached out and grabbed his neck, her hands suddenly glowing with raw magic. Her eyes widened in amazement when she saw the energy flowing from her. She'd only seen this happen once before, and that was when Grace had attacked James on the day he'd assaulted Gigi and tried to stop her from buying her house. She'd been certain that raw power had come from the Hannigan sisters who haunted Gigi's house, but now she wasn't so sure. Was it something all witches could tap but didn't realize it? Did they have to be pushed to a breaking point? Maybe. She didn't have time to think it over in that moment, but it was what she needed to defend herself and get back to Sebastian. "Take that, you utter piece of shit. You will not lay hands on me again."

James's eyes bugged out of his head, and his mouth opened, showing his teeth as he growled, "Fucking whore!" His veins popped out all over his skin as his muscles flexed beneath her grip. She held on tighter, determined to use as much of the raw magic as it took until she choked the evil right out of him.

"You can't do anything right, can you?" another male voice said from behind her just as something jabbed into her neck and her world went black.

CHAPTER TWENTY-FOUR

*G*igi's body felt like it was buried in sand. Her limbs were heavy, and her eyes were gritty when she tried to open them.

"Good afternoon, Clarity," a husky male voice said, making Gigi's ears ache.

She blinked again, trying to clear the grain from her eyes, and she squinted when the harsh light tried to blind her. "Where am I?' she asked in a raspy voice she didn't recognize.

"The headquarters for Mystical Finds of Avalon."

The words sent a shockwave through her, and she bolted upright, or at least tried to bolt upright. In reality, she pushed herself into a sitting position while gritting her teeth through the aches and pains that throbbed in her head, shoulder, and back. She felt like she'd been in a hit and run accident and left for dead. "Who are you? Emerson Sanders?"

The man chuckled. "Your mother would be so proud. You're smart, just like her."

"You knew my mother?" she asked with a gasp as her eyes

started to finally focus on the older man who was lounging in a red velvet armchair that matched the couch she was currently occupying. He was wearing a gray pin-striped suit and had jet-black hair that was obviously dyed. A person didn't acquire that many wrinkles and keep his natural hair color.

He let out a low chuckle, but didn't answer. Let's talk about you for a minute, Clarity Benson. Do you know why you're here?"

"No. And I go by Gigi now. Stop calling me Clarity," she ordered, acting as if she wasn't completely freaking out.

"Why? Clarity is a family name."

No it wasn't. At least not on her mother's side. She wasn't in the mood to argue with him. Nor did she care to tell him that her mother was the one who called her Gigi when she was little. After her mother's death, she took it on as a way to feel closer to her. "Because I like it better."

"I don't. You're still Clarity to me." He held up an art deco sapphire-and-diamond ring that looked exactly like her mother's.

Gigi glanced down at her naked finger and swallowed a cry of distress. He had her mother's ring. Likely, he knew what had happened to her mother. Fear and the instinct to flee warred with the desire to learn everything she could from him before she either escaped or met the same tragic fate as her mother. Answers. That was all she wanted in that moment. But she instinctively knew that she needed to remain strong in front of this man. Weakness was not an option.

"How is it that a ring I sold years ago ended up back in your possession?" He leaned forward, peering at her. "Did you track it down, or did you stumble upon it?"

"Why?"

"It will tell me a little something about you," he said, eyeing her intently.

Gigi didn't see a reason to lie to him. What difference did it make? "I just stumbled upon it at an estate sale."

His eyes glinted, and his lips turned up into a whisper of a smile. "That's interesting. Very interesting indeed."

"What's so interesting about that?" Whatever drug that had been injected into her veins was starting to fully wear off because she was fully awake now and full of so much rage her body was starting to tremble. "You know what? I don't care. Just give it back. I paid for that ring even after it was stolen from my mother."

"Oh, that's where you're mistaken, Clarity." He had a smug look on his face now. "This ring was given to me. And as for that money you have? Where exactly do you think it came from?" Sitting back in his chair, he rested one foot on his knee, acting as if he didn't have a care in the world as he waited for her response.

He wants to get a rise out of you. Don't give it to him.

Gigi stiffened. Was that her mom's voice? She wanted to call out, to ask the ghost if she really was her mother. But she couldn't. Not in front of Emerson. It would be a weakness she couldn't afford. The man had dropped two bombs in her lap, but she chose to focus on the most important one. Gigi forced a casual tone as she asked, "Care to explain how and when my mother gave you her ring?"

"She had a debt to pay." His narrowed eyes and curved lips projected an air of smugness that she'd like to smack right off his face.

"When?" Gigi asked, her tone cold. He was playing with her. That much was obvious. But what was it he wanted? To get a rise out of her, according to the voice she'd heard. So he wanted to rile her up, get her to fight back. She couldn't guarantee she wouldn't. That was just her nature. And as much as she'd let James dictate their lives for so long, she'd always had her limits.

"When what?" he taunted.

"When did she pay that debt?" Gigi leaned forward, staring him in the eye, determined to get the truth from this man.

"Oh, she didn't. All she did was buy time. Time's up now." He stood and using a remote, he made the gas fireplace come to life. He walked over and stood next to the hearth, studying the ring in the firelight. "You see, this ring, while it's special to you because your mother owned it, it's special to me because I gave it to her."

"No you didn't. My grandmother gave it to her the day I was born. And she set this one aside for me." Gigi held her other hand out, showing him the similar diamond-and-sapphire ring she always wore because she wanted to feel close to her family.

He shook his head and made a tsking sound. "So naïve. Poor child, there's a lot you don't know."

Gigi shook her head, tired of his games. "Perhaps. Maybe you should enlighten me."

He held the ring up again. "See this?"

"Yeah."

"This ring holds special powers. Or at least it does when it's being worn by a Benson witch. Where do you think that power came from that made it possible to nearly choke your husband to death?"

"What? That can't be right, I—" She stopped midsentence as she realized that he might be telling the truth. It would explain why she suddenly had powers she'd never had before.

"That's right, Clarity. This ring, the one I gave to her a few days after your birth, gave her the power of life. All those photography trips you thought she went on? They were to bring people back from the brink of death. She was a hero."

Gigi blinked at him, trying to process his words. "I don't understand. You're saying with this ring she could cure people who were terminally ill?"

"That's exactly what I'm saying."

"If all that's true, then why did she give the ring back to you?" Gigi didn't know if she believed him, but on the slim chance that he was telling the truth, she wanted—no needed—the entire story.

"The power isn't unlimited. It's not like she could've worked at a hospital and cured people all day every day. It took energy, and she needed to wait for that energy to replenish. That meant we needed to be discerning about who we chose to be given the gift of life."

"We? Are you saying you were a part of this?" Gigi was enthralled by the story, but her gut instinct was still telling her that something was terribly off. Her mother had gone missing, after all, and he'd somehow ended up with her ring. He knew what happened to her mother, and she was going to find out, sooner rather than later.

"I'm the one who vetted her clients. She took her orders from me."

"Orders? It sounds like you were forcing her to do something she didn't want to do," Gigi shot back.

He shrugged. "Sometimes, but it's the price she paid to keep me out of your life."

"Why would you want to be in my life? I don't—" She clamped her mouth shut as she recalled what he'd said. He'd given her mother the ring a few days after she was born. It was engraved with her birthday. Gigi felt like she was going to be sick. "This can't be real. Tell me you're not saying what I think you're saying."

"What is it you think I'm saying?" His amused tone pissed her off.

"You're saying you're my father, right? That's why you gave her the ring, and that's why she was trying to keep you away from me. But why? What's so terrible about you, other than abducting grown ass humans, that she didn't want you in my life?"

He chuckled. Actually chuckled as if any of this was funny. Her hands clenched, and she imagined sucker-punching him just before kneeing him in the balls. She already knew she hated this man and thanked the gods her mother had tried to protect her.

"Your mother didn't really care for my business principles," he said, staring into the fire. "I'll admit that some of my business arrangements are a little unsavory, but she didn't complain when I was flying her all over the world and showering her with gifts like this ring."

Had her mother really lived that life? Gigi thought of the trust fund money that was at her disposal. How her mother hadn't ever touched any of it and had instead lived a simple life near the beach. They hadn't had much in the way of luxuries, but she never recalled her mother being stressed about money or struggling to pay for basic needs. "What was the catalyst? Why did she leave you?"

"What makes you think she left me?" he asked.

"Because you said she paid a price to keep you away from me. I would assume she found something that she couldn't live with. Something that was so bad she had to keep you away to keep me safe."

He rolled his eyes. "It wasn't that terrible. For fuck's sake, you're just like your mother." He strode across the room and pulled a picture out of his desk. Emerson held it up, showing an older lady sitting in a rocker on a porch. Gigi squinted, looking at it closer.

"Is that Liza Crane?" Gigi asked, her entire body going cold. If he'd hurt Liza, she wasn't sure she was going to be able to control herself.

"Yes. It is. She was married to a man who was a gambling addict. He also worked for my company, and when he got into trouble, he stole from me. We gave him a specific amount of time to return the proprietary software, and when he didn't, two things happened: the man died and we went after all his assets, which left his wife with nothing."

"He died? How?" Gigi's heart raced as she waited for his response, knowing it had to have been the breaking point for her mother.

"He was beaten to death after he threatened to file a complaint against me and the company for human rights violations. We went after his wife to send a message." His tone was so matter of fact, so empty of emotion that it made Gigi's stomach roll. This man didn't have the capacity to love anyone. He was a sociopath.

Gigi swallowed the bile at the back of her throat. "So Mom left you, agreed to work for you to save people's lives, and all you had to do was stay out of mine. What happened when I was eighteen?" Gigi's voice grew stronger as she added, "How did you end up with the ring, and where is my mother?"

"After she found out that I refused her services to people who couldn't pay the fee, she accused me of playing God and told me that since you'd become an adult, she wouldn't be working for me anymore. But she didn't just want to walk away, she wanted to make sure no one else could profit like that again, so she used her magic to try to destroy the ring. Instead, it destroyed her. Sacrificed her. I'm sorry, Clarity, but your mother died by her own hand many years ago right there in Bellside, overlooking the sea."

CHAPTER TWENTY-FIVE

*G*igi's heart damned near exploded right in her chest. Hearing the words that her mother was dead, having it confirmed, was a pain so intense that she was having trouble breathing. Taking a shallow breath, she forced out, "Where is she? What did you do with her body?"

"Gone." A pained expression crossed his face and for a moment, Gigi thought maybe he was actually in pain at the thought of losing her. But then his face went blank as he added, "The magic turned her to dust. There never was a body to find. I'm sorry, Clarity. It isn't the ending I hoped for."

"Oh, it isn't?" Gigi jumped to her feet, unable to stop the pure rage coursing through her. "You forced her into a job she didn't want to do, one that was highly unethical, and when she tried to stop you, she died for it. But since it wasn't the ending you hoped for, you bear no responsibility, is that right?"

"I didn't kill her," he yelled back, his face red with anger. "You can try to blame me, but she's the one who tried to destroy that ring. She knew it's power, and still she threw everything she had into it. You can't blame me for that! I won't have it."

"Oh, you won't? What exactly are you going to do about it, *Dad*? Keep me locked in a gilded cage until I tell you it's not your fault?"

"Not a gilded one. But if you continue to be petulant, you won't be getting your freedom anytime soon." He walked over to the closed door. "Think about what you want out of life, Clarity. You can either agree to my request and go back to living in your quaint town in the house by the sea, or you can stay right here and do everything I ask of you or else life will get a lot worse."

Dread filled her gut as she asked the question she knew he'd been waiting for this entire time. "What is it you want from me?"

"I want you to take your mother's place. You'll wear the ring and cure those who can afford your treatment. You can either do that as a free woman or you can do it as a captive one. Your choice. Think it over." He pulled the door open and slipped out. There was no mistaking the click of the lock a second later.

Gigi let out the scream she'd been holding in and then collapsed back onto the red velvet couch. Her entire body was racked with sobs as she cried for her mother, for her sacrifice to keep Gigi safe, and finally for herself. For the situation she was in, the fact that her father was walking evil, and for the life she'd been building for herself that seemed to be crumbling around her.

* * *

GIGI DIDN'T KNOW how many hours had gone by. All she knew is that she was emotionally wrecked and exhausted beyond anything she'd felt before. She lay on that damned red couch, wondering what had happened to Sebastian. All she kept seeing was the man she loved unconscious on that beach. Had they taken him with them? Left him there? Was he even alive?

Her chest tightened again, but there were no more tears to shed. There was only dread left.

The door creaked open, and before she even looked up, she knew it was Emerson. There was a presence about him that made her skin crawl. It was as if her DNA sensed his, and it made her want to try to get as far away from him as possible.

"Have you made a decision?" Emerson asked.

"The answer is no," she said without any heat or passion. She'd gone dead inside, too spent from the grief of the confirmation of her mother's death.

"Are you sure about that?" he asked. Light flickered from the other side of the room, drawing Gigi's attention.

The monitor on a desk had come to life and a video was playing. The camera scanned a simple room that had a twin bed and nothing else other than a dark-haired man who was sitting against the wall, holding his head in his bloody hands.

Gigi sat up, giving the video her full attention. She knew those hands, blood and all. "Sebastian," she whispered. Then she glared at Emerson. "What have you done to him?"

"Nothing. He spent over an hour pounding on the door." Emerson sat on the edge of the desk and studied her. "I dare say you have better coping skills than the attorney. His anger isn't going to help his cause."

"Why is he here? Why did James drug him? And why did James bring us here?" she demanded, never taking her eyes off the man she loved.

"James works for me. I hired him the day you turned eighteen to keep an eye on you and to report back about your life. Just because I promised your mother I'd stay away, that didn't mean I wasn't going to keep checking on you. You are a Sanders, even if your birth certificate says Benson." He gave her what she assumed was his idea of a loving smile. It made her skin crawl. Who hired people to spy on their kid?

"So my marriage to James was a complete lie? He only did it because he worked for you?" The thought made her want to jump out of her skin. The violation was so revolting, she had trouble quantifying it.

He shrugged. "I'm sure James enjoyed your family trust. There were perks to being Mr. Clarity Martin. When you threw him out, he moved on to my other daughter. I think you know Autumn."

Gigi nodded. She'd made the connection earlier, but hadn't had the energy to think about the fact that she apparently had a half sister who may or may not have known about her all along.

"He thought she was coming into some money. When I corrected him, he bailed quickly. Autumn made her choices, so her trust was dissolved. He didn't realize that." He shook his head in disgust. "Real piece of work, that one. Did you know he blew his entire divorce settlement investing in a knock-off Tiger King show? This one featured beavers and a washed-up former child actor and his two cougar lovers. The show was canceled before it ever aired. He's a real idiot."

"And yet, he apparently still works for you," Gigi bit out, not at all surprised James had tried his hand at Hollywood. He'd always wanted to be someone important in the industry.

"He has his uses. When I learned you had found the ring, I sent him to keep an eye on you. Then I started to think that it was awfully curious that the ring found its way back to you. And I started to wonder, what if? All he was supposed to do was bring you to me so I could find out if the ring was genuine. But he's even too incompetent for that. I had to send one of my goons to clean up his mess. Not all is lost, though. Both of you are here, and I find that very useful." Emerson's gaze landed on the ring in his palm. "I never imagined this thing would recharge. If I'd known that, I never would've sold it."

Gigi didn't respond to his ramblings. Her gaze was fixed on Sebastian. He looked so broken sitting there in that bare room, no doubt going crazy wondering what had happened to her. She wanted to reach out, to touch him through the screen as if that was even possible. But she wouldn't show vulnerability like that to Emerson Sanders. She'd already worked out that he thrived on the pain of others.

"Let Sebastian go. He's not involved in this," Gigi said, her voice far too hoarse.

Emerson laughed. "No? I'd say he's right in the middle of it since he'd do just about anything to find you right about now." He pursed his lips in thought. "But there is one way I'll let him go. Say you'll work for me and both of you can be free to live your lives however you want. You'll, of course, need to be available when we have clients, but you don't work, so that shouldn't be an issue."

Gigi cut her gaze to him, glaring at him. He was insane if he thought Sebastian was just going to let this go without pressing charges.

"I know what you're thinking, but trust me, I'm well versed on just how far a man will go to protect the woman he loves. If your life depends on his silence, he'll do what he has to."

"You have no idea what I'm thinking," she lied.

He stared her down and then shook his head before retreating again. "I'll give you time to think about your options."

She watched as he left the room and wasn't surprised to hear the lock click. She glanced around the room, looking for the camera. If Sebastian was being recorded, she had to assume she was, too. The room was set up as a parlor, with fancy velvet furniture, wood paneling on the walls, and an expensive rug. But other than the monitor, there wasn't much else.

Gigi rose and swayed on her feet. When was the last time she'd eaten? She had no idea. But she was thirsty, and her head was swimming with dizziness. She had to get out of there before she got any weaker. Full of rage over what they'd done to Sebastian and the fact that her marriage had been even more of a sham than she'd imagined, she hurried over to the other side of the room. After yanking the heavy red drapes aside, she let out a cry of frustration when she found solid walls instead of the windows she'd been expecting.

"Dammit!" she yelled, pounding on the solid paneling. Her knees buckled, and she slid to the floor, her fight gone. There was nothing to do but wait.

CHAPTER TWENTY-SIX

*G*igi had gone over the plan in her head over a hundred times. As soon as Emerson came back, she was going to make her move. Earlier that morning, food had arrived along with a set of silverware. She'd eaten, because she had to in order to restore her strength, and then done as she was told and left the tray by the door.

A young woman had collected it, checked to make sure the silverware had been returned, and then deliberately dropped the fork onto the floor before leaving. She hadn't looked at her, but there'd been no mistaking that she'd meant for the fork to fall. Gigi wasn't going to waste her chance.

She had to wonder if that scene had been caught on tape. She wasn't sure, because the fork was sort of behind the desk, so she'd been careful about retrieving it. First, she'd pounded on the door, demanding to be let out, though she knew that was futile. She'd already tried that. But then she'd lowered herself so that her back was resting against the wall, and it was easy to collect the fork without it being obvious. She just had to hope for the best.

Then she waited. And waited some more. And waited some more. Her butt was numb, and her legs periodically fell asleep, but she wasn't moving. Not until someone came back.

Finally, after what seemed like days but was likely only a few hours, she heard the lock click.

Gigi jumped up, nearly collapsing as one knee complained, but she grabbed the door frame to keep herself steady. As soon as the door swung open, she hurled herself at her intruder with everything she had.

"Fuck!" Hope cried as she jerked back, the fork lodged in her biceps.

"Oh my god!" Gigi cried. "What are you doing here?"

"Saving your ass. Thanks for the forking." She glanced at the utensil sticking out of her flesh and then yanked it out. Blood started running down her arm, but she ignored it. "Come on. There's no time to waste." She grabbed Gigi's hand and ran full speed through a giant mansion that was full of useless, expensive things. They were closing in on a hallway when Hope said, "Hurry. We're almost there."

Gigi was still exhausted. Her legs burned, and her vision was blurry, but her coven had arrived and that alone had given her the energy boost she needed to make it out of there. But she couldn't just leave without Sebastian.

"Wait!" She grabbed Hope's wrist, stopping her. "Sebastian is here. We can't leave without him."

"We know," she said. "Grace and Joy went after him."

Grace and Joy? How much harder was it for them to get to him than it had been for Hope to find her? It wasn't the time to ask, though. She took off after Hope, who was gesturing for her to exit through a side door.

The harsh afternoon sun nearly blinded Gigi, but she squinted through it and kept running... right into the solid form of one of Emerson's goons. Gigi fell backward, landing with a thud on her backside. "Oomph!"

Beside her, Hope was struggling to get free from the goon's twin. He had one arm twisted behind her back, and Gigi had déjà vu from when James had captured her the same way. Only Hope did some fancy move and immediately freed herself then knocked her guy on his ass.

Gigi snapped out of her mental trance and focused on the guy above her who was reaching for her. She saw her opening and took it, kicking him in the head with one foot and then the other, giving it everything she had. He fell to the right, completely knocked out. "Let's get out of here," she cried to Hope as they both took off again.

Hope led her to a gate in the compound, and they were just about to slip through when the first shot was fired.

They both flung themselves to the ground and scrambled to hide behind a flower box.

"Freeze," Emerson said, his voice harsh and full of authority.

Gigi glanced up to see him holding Sebastian in front of him, a gun pointed at his head.

"You know I'll do it. Your choice, Clarity. Go back into the mansion without a fight, or I'll kill your boyfriend right here in front of you."

Gigi slowly got to her feet, her hands raised over her head. Her entire body was shaking, and she thought her heart would explode from fear. "Don't hurt him. I'll do whatever you want."

"No, Gigi," Sebastian rasped out. "I will not let you be his prisoner."

She met Sebastian's eyes and saw love and devotion staring back at her. He meant it. He was willing to die to save her from her father. There was only one problem with that; she wasn't willing to sacrifice him. He was the only man she'd ever loved, and after all these years, she wasn't going to lose him like this. "I won't let him do it," she told Sebastian. "Please, just accept that this is my choice."

"Gigi," he whispered, shaking his head.

"It's not just him you have to think about," Emerson growled. "Your little friends are locked in his room. If you leave, you'll be sacrificing them too."

"If you touch Grace or Joy, you'll answer to me, old man," Hope said. Her fists were clenched, and her face was full of fury. Gigi had no doubt she'd get her revenge if Emerson made good on his promise. But she wasn't going to let it get that far. She had to try, because she knew with complete certainty that even if she did agree to go along with Emerson's plan, to give herself up for the ones she loved, he would never let them go. Not now that they had infiltrated his compound and knew what he was capable of. He'd have to cover his tracks.

"Fine. I'll go with you. Just don't hurt them. I'll work for you, go wherever you want. But only if you promise to let them go," she said earnestly.

"Will you sign a magically binding contract?" he asked, one eyebrow raised.

"No, she won't, you manipulative piece of shit," Hope spat out.

"I'm not talking to you, Ms. Anderson. Kindly keep your big trap shut before someone gets hurt," Emerson said, never taking his eyes off of Gigi.

"You—" Hope started.

"Please, Hope. Let me handle this," Gigi said as she moved toward Emerson. "Let me keep you all safe. That's all I want."

Her father's lips curved into a self-satisfied smile, and Gigi knew she had him. He believed she was giving everything up for those she loved, just like her mother had. But Gigi had weapons her mother hadn't been lucky enough to have. A coven who didn't take shit from anyone and a man who loved her so completely that he'd give his life for hers.

"Let him go, and I'll sign the contract," Gigi said.

"The contract first." Emerson waved the gun at her, and that was his fatal mistake, because Sebastian moved quicker than she'd ever seen him move. One second he was in a choke hold with a gun on him, and in the next he had his hand around Emerson's wrist, trying to squeeze so hard that the man had no choice but to drop the gun.

But Emerson was stronger than he looked, and the two appeared to be in an evenly matched battle, each struggling to gain dominance over the other.

"Gigi, let's go. It's what Sebastian wants," Hope said in her ear, trying to pull her away out of the range of the gun.

"No. I'm not leaving him."

"Son of a... all right. I'm not leaving you, either, so let's do this," Hope said as she grabbed both of Gigi's hands and started to chant a ritual designed to manifest rain.

"Rain?" Gigi asked.

"Trust me," she said and went back to chanting. Gigi immediately joined in, and something strange happened. Her hands started to glow with magic just as they had when she'd been wearing her mother's ring.

Hope jumped back, wincing in pain just as Gigi lunged at Emerson, unleashing all of her magic on the man who'd spent the last two days torturing her and Sebastian. His body went rigid and the gun fired. Emerson and Sebastian both crumpled to the ground. Gigi went with them, her hands still grasping Emerson. His body twitched, and he tried helplessly to dislodge himself from her grip, but the magic was too powerful.

Gigi got on her knees and stared down into the old man's eyes, watching as the light slowly drained from them. "You know all those people you fleeced when they were on their death beds? This is for them, you evil piece of garbage." She unleashed as much of the magic as she could muster, reveling in the act of ending the man who had taken her mother from her.

"Gigi, stop," Sebastian said, his voice distant to her ears. So distant that she didn't even acknowledge him.

"Don't become what he is, love. Please," Sebastian said. "Look at me. I need you to look at me." The waning strength in his words were finally what got her to shift her gaze to the man lying a foot away from them.

"Don't let him make you into something you're not," Sebastian said, his breathing haggard and thready.

Gigi finally took a good look at him and spotted Hope trying to staunch a blood stain on his chest. He'd been shot when she'd attacked Emerson. "Oh my god, Sebastian. No. God no." Tears streamed down her face as she watched his skin go pale in the sunlight.

He reached out and touched her face. "I have always loved you."

It was a goodbye. He was leaving her. And there was nothing she could do... or was there? Gigi turned her attention back to Emerson's lifeless body. He was still breathing, but he wasn't conscious. At least he wouldn't be putting up a fight. She frantically searched for the ring she knew he kept in his right pocket. It was always the same. Front right pocket. And sure enough, as soon as she stuffed her hand in the right pocket, her fingers closed around it.

Without wasting any time, Gigi shoved the ring on her right ring finger, exactly where her mother had worn it, and then she placed her hands on Sebastian's chest. She had no idea how to do this, but she would not lose him without a fight.

Gigi closed her eyes, thought of her mother, and prayed for guidance.

Pour your love into the magic, Clarity. It will be all right. Just let the energy flow from you to Sebastian. That's it. You've got it. Now, let go.

Gigi didn't know she was sobbing until she opened her blurry eyes and saw a fuzzy, but smiling Sebastian right in front of her. "I'm so sorry," she said. "This shouldn't have—"

"Shh." He placed a hand over hers. "No apologies. You saved me. You saved us all."

"I think it's the other way around, but we can argue about that later," she said and bent over to kiss him softly on the lips. "I love you."

His eyes fluttered closed as he whispered, "I love you, too."

Sirens wailed in the background, and it was music to her ears. She glanced at Hope. "Will you stay with him? I'm going to go find Grace and Joy."

"We're right here, Gigi," Grace said from behind her. When Gigi twisted her head, she found her two friends with a man who looked just as haggard at they did. "We found Gage, Sebastian's PI, too. They had him locked up in a shitty room with nothing, not even a bed."

All three were slightly bruised and a little rough around the edges, but they were whole and that was all that mattered. "Thank the gods. And thank you for finding us."

"We didn't," Grace said. "It was Autumn."

Gigi glanced around. "Where is she?"

"Inside still." Grace kneeled beside Gigi and placed a hand

on her shoulder. "Autumn's in pretty bad shape, but I think she'll be okay once she gets medical attention."

"What happened?" Gigi asked, almost afraid to hear the answer.

Joy took a step forward, and that's when Gigi realized there was blood all over her jeans. "She's been shot twice. Once in the shoulder, the other her thigh. Her father did it because she let us in to get you out."

Gigi glanced between Sebastian and the house, torn about what to do. She desperately wanted to be in both places at once. "Whose watching over her?" she asked.

"Her girlfriend," Joy said.

"Go. I'll be fine," Sebastian said, staring up at Gigi. He gave her a weak smile as he added, "The ambulance is coming, and the coven is here to take care of me."

She gave him another quick kiss, and then took off into the house.

Gigi found the young woman who'd dropped the fork she'd ended up using on Hope kneeling over Autumn in the foyer. Autumn was pale as a ghost, shivering, and covered in blood, but it looked like the bleeding was under control. Gigi dropped to her knees on the other side of her half sister, grabbed her free hand, and held it in both of hers. "You're going to be okay, you know that, right?"

Autumn nodded. "That's what Zoe keeps telling me." She cut her gaze to the younger woman, who had a calm expression on her face and an easy smile for Autumn.

"It's the truth," Zoe said. "I'm really good at what I do."

"She's a paramedic. Deals with crazier shit than this all the time," Autumn said in a halting voice.

"Just relax, baby. That's the shock that's making you stutter like that." She glanced at the door and tightened her grip on Autumn's hand.

"I can help," Gigi said. "It's magic. Are you okay with that?"

Autumn looked at Zoe for an answer.

"What kind of magic?" Zoe asked.

"Healing energy."

Zoe's eyes widened. "Hell yes. I've never seen it in action before."

Gigi glanced at Autumn. "Are you okay with this?"

She nodded and closed her eyes, still shivering.

"Stay calm, pour your love into the energy," Gigi told herself. She thought of soothing things, sunshine and joy and blue skies and puppies and rainbows as she focused on sending positive light into Autumn.

When she finally released the magic, she glanced down at her half sister and was pleased to see that her coloring was better and she'd stopped shivering.

Thank you, Zoe mouthed before she bent down to whisper something in Autumn's ear.

Gigi stood just as the paramedics arrived and started loading Autumn onto a stretcher. Certain that she was in good hands, she made her way back outside, intending to go to the hospital with Sebastian. But instead, she found herself face-to-face with a very unhappy detective.

"Ms. Martin, we're going to need to have a word with you," the woman said.

"Yes. Of course." She stared longingly at the ambulance they'd just loaded Sebastian into and then followed the detective inside the house and showed her the room where she'd been held captive.

Hours later, Gigi finally made it to the hospital. She stood in the doorway of Sebastian's room while she waited for the doctor to finish reading his charts.

When Sebastian's heartrate spiked, the doctor turned, spotted her, and started to chuckle. "Looks like someone is feeling better already." She gestured for Gigi to enter and then said, "I'll be back before my shift's over to check on you again, but it looks like you're going to be fine. Thanks to your girlfriend here, you're probably looking at an accelerated recovery rate. Instead of a few months, it'll probably be more like a few weeks."

"Thanks, doc," Sebastian said, smiling at Gigi.

"I'm going to stay after visiting hours," Gigi told the doctor.

She laughed. "Since it's already after hours, I assumed that was the case. Just let him get some rest and it'll be fine."

Gigi nodded her thanks and made her way over to Sebastian. She clasped his hand in hers and asked, "How are you?"

"Better now that you're here." He scooted over and patted the bed. "Sit here. I want to feel you next to me."

"Are you sure I won't hurt you?"

He shook his head. "Thanks to whatever magic you infused me with and that pain killer they gave me an hour ago, I'm pain free."

That was really something considering he'd been shot. Gigi crawled onto the bed and cuddled up next to him, careful to not bother the wound on his opposite shoulder. Once his arm was around her, she let out a tired sigh of relief and asked, "Will you move in with me?"

"Yes." He kissed the top of her head and tightened his hold on her.

"Just like that?" She glanced up at his tired face. "You can think about it, or even just say no if you think it's too fast. Or—"

"Gigi," he said softly. "I've been in love with you for over twenty years. It's not too fast."

She chuckled. "Well, when you put it that way... I'll get a key made for you tomorrow."

"Good."

They lay together, just silently holding each other for a long time until Sebastian said, "Thank you."

"For what?" she asked, not sure she deserved any thanks at all. It was her fault he'd been drugged, held captive, and shot.

"For choosing love rather than revenge. It matters. You know that, right?"

She nodded, tears stinging her eyes again. "He's in custody. The detective is certain he'll be denied bail."

"That's good news."

"They arrested James too. They found him hiding in a closet. The coward. He tried to tell them he was held captive, too, but Emerson was a video creep. Every room was being taped. There's a mountain of evidence. Between that and the ring..." Her voice cracked on a sob. "It's possible Emerson will go down for my mother's murder. As for James, he's looking at accessory and abduction charges. Maybe some fraud since he married me under false pretenses."

Sebastian gathered her close with his good arm and held her as she cried again for the loss of her mother, for the ordeal they'd been put through, and for the fact they'd made it out alive and together.

"It's going to get better now, Gigi. Now that you have answers and James is out of your life, you can truly move on. I can't wait to see where you go from here."

She smiled up at him. "Wherever I go, it's going to be with you."

"Pure cheese. I love it."

Gigi laughed and knew that even though she still had issues to sort through, he was right. Her past was finally behind her, and she was ready to look forward to the future. "You love my cheese?"

"No doubt about it. Now give me some cheddar before I lose my mind."

Grinning like a fool, Gigi lifted her lips to his and kissed him until the heart monitor beat so fast the nurse came in to break them up.

CHAPTER TWENTY-SEVEN

"Cheers!" Gigi raised her champagne glass in the air, toasting with Skyler and Carly Preston on their epic sales from the grand opening. The soft opening had been a month ago, and although a quieter affair after everything that had gone down at Emerson's, the event had been very promising.

"I can't believe we sold out of the cellulite cream," Carly said, eyeing the display as if a stray jar might pop out of nowhere. The movie star was wearing the most gorgeous white dress with an off-white lily pattern covering it. As soon as Gigi had spotted her, she'd run to Skyler and demanded he find her something decent to wear. He'd come through, of course, with an off-the-shoulder red gown that made her look like the movie star's younger sister. It was amazing.

"I can. Did you see what a phenomenal job Hope did of filling this space with women over forty?" Gigi said. "I swear, it looked like a retirement party in here."

Skyler laughed. "Do not let any of them hear you say that, or we'll be out of business in less than five seconds."

Gigi snickered. "I'm just joking. Listen, I'm in that group. And I have two jars of Carly's miracle cream at home. One can never be too prepared."

Carly shook her head at their antics. "I'm glad it's a success, but I'm going to be really busy trying to fill all these orders."

"We need a production facility," Gigi said. "Because I'm in the same boat. And I even made extra, thinking I was ahead of the game."

"You know what," Carly said, tapping a red fingernail against her lips. "I think we need to really consider that. And if we did that, we could expand and sell our products all over."

Skyler cleared his throat. "Um, I don't mean to be a buzzkill, but you guys do know my store has exclusivity within fifty miles, right?"

Carly rolled her eyes at him. "Of course I do. I mean we could sell this stuff at spas and other specialty shops across the country. And maybe keep some extra special stuff just for our favorite boy, so he can market them as exclusive on the website."

"Oh, I'm liking this. Go on," Skyler said. The three of them talked about logistics, where they might find a production facility, and how they'd go about running it so that neither Carly nor Gigi had to be there full time.

"Excuse me." Iris Hartsen, the town's mayor, stopped to stand between Gigi and Carly. "I hope you don't mind me butting in, but I overheard you talking about finding a production facility for your wonderful skin care products. If you're serious about opening one, I know the perfect place just outside of town. It's currently being used to produce cosmetics, but it's shutting down next month."

"Why?" Gigi asked.

"Relocating overseas," she said with a sigh. "It's tough to

keep jobs at home when corporations don't care about much other than their stockholders."

Gigi shared a glance with Carly, who nodded.

"It sounds pretty good," Gigi said. "We'd love to take a look at it as soon as that's a possibility."

"Perfect," Iris said, adjusting her fitted suit jacket as if she'd just won a prize. It made Gigi chuckle to herself, but she supposed it was a good thing to have a mayor who cared so much about the town that she was always on the lookout for opportunities for new businesses and new jobs.

As Iris and Skyler talked shop about the downtown retail spaces, Gigi scanned the crowd. Sebastian was having a drink with Hope and Lucas, but he wasn't paying any attention to them. He was watching her. Her entire body warmed from his gaze. As soon as he'd gotten out of the hospital, he'd moved into her house. Since he'd just been renting a place for the summer, it hadn't been much, but they'd already decided he would be moving to Premonition Pointe permanently. He'd just work remotely and travel to his job when needed.

Gigi was surprised at how easy of a transition it had been. Although the therapist she was seeing hadn't been surprised at all. She'd said that other than her mom, Sebastian was the only true family Gigi had ever had. It made sense that there wasn't any awkwardness. They knew each other too well for that.

"Hey, sis. You know, you look pretty silly standing here by yourself, gawking at that gorgeous attorney of yours," Autumn said, slipping her arm around Gigi's waist.

Gigi smiled at her sister. Sebastian might have been the only family she'd known, but the one good thing that came out of discovering Emerson Sanders was her father was learning that she and Autumn really were half sisters.

Autumn hadn't had a clue that they were related. She'd

been shocked and confused and really upset that her father hadn't told her she had a sister. But when the shock faded, she was elated, and it hadn't taken long for the two of them to become close. So close that they even sometimes did therapy together. When Autumn had suggested it, Gigi didn't think it was a great idea at first, but when they realized they were both working through a lot of the same stuff, it just made sense. If Gigi was honest, those sessions were the ones where she grew the most.

"I can't help it. He's just too pretty," Gigi said.

Autumn sighed and batted her eyelashes as she made googly eyes in his direction. "You're right. He's dreamy."

Gigi grinned at her antics. "Now go make those eyes at Zoe before she feels slighted."

Autumn glanced over at her girlfriend, who had been on Pete's arm most of the evening. The boutique had just been so busy, there hadn't been time for any of them to spend time with their dates. It was a good problem to have. "She really looks gorgeous, doesn't she?"

Zoe was dressed in a slim cut velvet suit and had a royal blue silk shirt peeking out of the jacket. Gigi nodded her agreement. "She's stunning. And smart. Keep her, okay?"

"I'm planning on it." Autumn winked at Gigi and made a beeline for her girlfriend.

Ever since Emerson had been arrested, Autumn had come out of her shell. She was no longer Skyler's quiet sidekick. She was more like the superhero who made everything happen at Sky's The Limit. She'd been on her own for years after leaving her father's company and being cut off financially, but something had still been holding her back. It turned out to be leftover issues about her father. She'd shed that cloak since starting therapy, and Gigi was thrilled to see it.

Gigi was about to go for another glass of champagne when she spotted Grace, Hope, and Joy coming for her. She grinned at them and held her arms out for a hug. They fell into her and the four of them wrapped their arms around each other as her coven mates congratulated her on her skin care success.

"Thanks," Gigi said. "But I couldn't have done it without you three talking it up all night."

Grace waved a dismissive hand. "Please, that stuff is genius. We were thrilled to help."

The four of them chatted for a few minutes and planned their next coven meeting on the bluff.

"I was thinking about inviting Carly," Joy said. "What do you think?"

"Yes," the other three chimed in immediately.

"Perfect. We'll initiate her next week," Joy said. "After we're done with our shoot."

"Shoot?" Gigi asked. "Did you get another role?"

Joy nodded vigorously. "It's a weekly drama that Carly is starring in for one of the streaming channels, and when one of the actresses dropped out, Carly recommended me. I got the call today. I start Monday!"

There was a collective shout of delight, and they all had far too many rounds of champagne. Gigi was certain she'd pay for that in the morning, but it was worth it. By the time Sebastian was driving Gigi home, she was exhausted and happier than she'd ever been.

"It was a great night," Sebastian said as he pulled into the driveway.

"The best," she agreed.

As they walked to the door, he pulled her in close and said, "It's about to get even better."

"Promise?" She smiled up at him, her heart fuller than she could ever remember.

"Always." He kissed her tenderly, and then as it always did, their kiss quickly turned heated.

Gigi pulled back and said, "I love you, Sebastian Knight."

His dark eyes, so full of love, searched hers as he said, "Enough to marry me?"

A slow grin claimed Gigi's lips as she nodded and asked, "What took you so long?"

CHAPTER TWENTY-EIGHT

*I*ris Hartsen was having a bad week. A very bad week. After attending three new business openings and making connections for real industry growth, Iris had been called into work on a Saturday and presented with a letter from the town council asking her to resign her post. The letter had described the rising rate of violent crime and her husband's involvement in a drug trafficking scheme. It didn't matter that she'd thrown him out and divorced him the minute she'd learned about his crimes last fall. But they were only concerned that Tom had gotten off on a technicality, and they thought Iris engineered it.

She let out a humorless bark of laughter. In the immortal words of Cher Horowitz, *As if!*

If someone had asked her a year ago what her husband was like, she'd have said kind, funny, loyal, a good businessman, and a contender for the most supportive husband of the year award. Now? Cheater, thief, criminal, and the guy who'd gotten her ousted from the job she loved. She hated that he wasn't paying for his crimes. The judge had let him go with a warning that if he ended up in her court again, she'd find a reason to give him time. It had been unprofessional, but Iris understood the judge was just as pissed as she was about the lack of accountability.

"Fucking piece of toad slime," Iris said.

"You're not talking to me, are you?" a man from next door asked.

Iris glanced over and spotted her new neighbor smiling at her, humor dancing in his brilliant blue eyes. "Not yet, but give it a few minutes. You never know how this conversation is going to go."

He chuckled. "Oh, yeah. I'm going to like you."

She snorted out a laugh. "We'll see."

"I hope so. Actually, I was just going to come over and ask if you have any coffee. It turns out I'm a shit shopper and forgot to pick some up yesterday, and I could really use a shot of caffeine."

"Sorry. Fresh out." She actually had emergency instant, but there was no way she was letting the handsome stranger know she drank that stuff when she was too busy to make a pot.

"Out of coffee. Damn. We're pathetic. In that case, get your shoes on and let me take you to the café on the corner. It looks like we could both use a pick-me-up."

Iris stared at him, torn between being amused and annoyed. She'd been minding her own business, stewing about the shit going down in her life, when he'd interrupted her and, dammit, made her laugh. The nerve of him.

Her neighbor disappeared into his house but returned less than a minute later with a small fluffy dog on a leash.

That did it. She was a sucker for dogs. "Give me a second." Iris ran into her house, finger-combed her wavy blond hair, and stuffed her feet into a pair of walking shoes. When she returned to her porch, she was greeted by a jumping, happy dog. "What's your name, sweetheart?"

"Kade," her neighbor said.

Gigi glanced up. "Your dog with a pink collar is named Kade?"

"Oh, you were calling BeeBee sweetheart? My mistake." He smirked at her and held his hand out. "I'm Kade Carson. And this is Bunny, also known as BeeBee and Buster, depending on my mood. Usually it's BeeBee."

"Uh, okay. That was a lot all at once." She shook his hand. "Iris Hartsen. No pets, but I'm pleased to meet BeeBee. You should take her to Four Paws Barkery for a special treat. She'd love it." She squatted down and let the fluffy dog love all over her for a minute.

"No doubt about that. We'll check it out. Thanks." He fell into step beside her with BeeBee leading the way. "You have recs for a Barkery, but no pets? Looks like that's a mistake that needs to be rectified."

"Why? Because everyone needs a dog?" she asked.

"No, because you clearly love them. Tell the truth, now. You wouldn't be here with me right now if she hadn't come with us, would you?"

Iris laughed again. Dammit, how did this guy do that? "Probably not. And you're right. I do love dogs, but my life has been too busy. No time for a dog." At least she hadn't *had* time for a dog, but now she would, wouldn't she? Maybe it was time to take a trip to Puppy Love, the local animal shelter.

"And now you're thinking about adopting one, right?" he said, grinning at her.

"Do you read minds or something?" she demanded.

This time he laughed. "No. But I'm good at reading people, and it's written all over your face."

She let out an irritated huff.

"But really, if you're not ready, don't do it. I'm just teasing. Besides, now that I'm your neighbor, I'm sure BeeBee would love to visit any time you need a puppy fix."

"Looks like someone needs a puppy sitter," she teased.

"Busted." They talked easily and teased each other all the way to the coffee shop. By the time she had a latte in her hand, Iris was more relaxed than she'd been in years.

Then the strangest thing happened. A loud boom sounded over the town, and just like that, all the tourists vanished right into thin air. It was like a ghost town or like aliens had come down and snatched the entire temporary population.

Kade stood still, staring at Main Street and then at Iris. "What the fuck just happened?"

"It's a curse," Iris said, her skin itching with the irritating residue of a powerful spell. "Someone or something just cursed Premonition Pointe."

"What?" he asked.

"I have to go." Iris tossed her latte and took off running. Ten minutes later, she was standing at Grace Valentine's door, ringing the bell repeatedly until the other woman finally answered.

"Iris. What's wrong?"

"The town has been cursed. I need the coven's help."

DEANNA'S BOOK LIST

Witches of Keating Hollow:

Soul of the Witch

Heart of the Witch

Spirit of the Witch

Dreams of the Witch

Courage of the Witch

Love of the Witch

Power of the Witch

Essence of the Witch

Muse of the Witch

Vision of the Witch

Waking of the Witch

Witches of Christmas Grove:

A Witch For Mr. Holiday

A Witch For Mr. Christmas

A Witch For Mr. Winter

Premonition Pointe Novels:
Witching For Grace
Witching For Hope
Witching For Joy
Witching For Clarity
Witching For Moxie
Witching For Kismet

Jade Calhoun Novels:
Haunted on Bourbon Street
Witches of Bourbon Street
Demons of Bourbon Street
Angels of Bourbon Street
Shadows of Bourbon Street
Incubus of Bourbon Street
Bewitched on Bourbon Street
Hexed on Bourbon Street
Dragons of Bourbon Street

Pyper Rayne Novels:
Spirits, Stilettos, and a Silver Bustier
Spirits, Rock Stars, and a Midnight Chocolate Bar
Spirits, Beignets, and a Bayou Biker Gang
Spirits, Diamonds, and a Drive-thru Daiquiri Stand
Spirits, Spells, and Wedding Bells

Ida May Chronicles:
Witched To Death
Witch, Please
Stop Your Witchin'

Crescent City Fae Novels:

Influential Magic
Irresistible Magic
Intoxicating Magic

Last Witch Standing:
Bewitched by Moonlight
Soulless at Sunset
Bloodlust By Midnight
Bitten At Daybreak

Witch Island Brides:
The Wolf's New Year Bride
The Vampire's Last Dance
The Warlock's Enchanted Kiss
The Shifter's First Bite

Destiny Novels:
Defining Destiny
Accepting Fate

Wolves of the Rising Sun:
Jace
Aiden
Luc
Craved
Silas
Darien
Wren

Black Bear Outlaws:
Cyrus
Chase

Cole

Bayou Springs Alien Mail Order Brides:
Zeke
Gunn
Echo

ABOUT THE AUTHOR

New York Times and USA Today bestselling author, Deanna Chase, is a native Californian, transplanted to the slower paced lifestyle of southeastern Louisiana. When she isn't writing, she is often goofing off with her husband in New Orleans or playing with her two shih tzu dogs. For more information and updates on newest releases visit her website at deannachase.com.